DEAD TO THE WORLD
CROSSROADS QUEEN
BOOK 1

ANNABEL CHASE

RED PALM PRESS LLC

Copyright © 2023 by Annabel Chase

All rights reserved.

No part of this book may be reproduced in any form or by any electronic or mechanical means, including information storage and retrieval systems, without written permission from the author, except for the use of brief quotations in a book review.

Cover by Trif Designs

Created with Vellum

CHAPTER 1

"You're doing it wrong."

I stopped hammering long enough to cast a sharp eye at the apparition behind me. "I know how to use a hammer."

"Could've fooled me. Your grip looks weak. You need to strengthen your wrists."

With a deep sigh, I set the hammer on the table. There'd be no peace until I let this one feel useful; I could sense it. "Go on then, Roy. Dazzle me with your insight."

"I told you, the name's Ray. I'm not trying to mansplain or anything disrespectful like that. It's just that I spent years as a carpenter, and it's downright painful to watch you work." The ghost drifted to stand opposite me. He was a burly man in dungarees and a red plaid shirt. It wouldn't surprise me to learn he'd been buried with his beloved toolkit.

"And how many years ago was that?" Ray looked to be in his early eighties.

"Carpentry isn't like technology. Nothing much changes." He tried to lift the hammer, but his hand swiped through it. "You'll have to pretend I'm holding it."

I watched as the ghost demonstrated his technique, which,

to be perfectly honest, wasn't very different from the way my grandfather had taught me. I could've given him hints on how to make contact with physical objects, but that would only encourage him to hang around. "Thank you. That's helpful, Roy."

"My name is Ray. Sweet Nellie, I swear you're saying Roy on purpose."

He wasn't wrong, and I was willing to do a lot worse to preserve my peace. When I first moved in six months ago, I helped the majority of the residents in the adjacent cemetery cross over, except for two that declined so respectfully, I couldn't bring myself to force them. Personally, I didn't see the appeal of sticking around. The sleepy town of Fairhaven was hardly a hotbed of excitement, not that they could travel beyond the gate anyway—which was probably the reason this ghost had taken a keen interest in my chores.

"Thank you, Ray." I picked up the hammer, keeping my gaze fixed on the ghost. "You realize you've broken the first rule, right?" After helping the other spirits cross over, I'd given the remaining stage five clingers my rules. Rule 1: No entering the house without permission.

"I know, but it gets dull as dishwater out there," Ray complained.

"Then cross over." Whack! The nail slid into place.

"Don't want to."

"Why not?"

Ray fell silent.

I twisted to look at him. "Listen, I don't know if you realize this, but I can make you leave here."

"Then why don't you?"

"Because I believe you're entitled to free will and bodily autonomy, even in your current state."

"You're one of those feminists, huh?"

"I am, indeed."

"I've got a few of them in my family. Strongest Black

women you'll ever meet." His chin lifted. "My grandbaby Alicia is…"

I put on a set of headphones, hopeful Ray would get the hint. When I looked up a few minutes later, he was gone.

I continued hammering until my eyes blurred. This task was one of about two thousand. It was my own fault, of course. I bought a house that had a date with a wrecking ball until I stepped in. If only I had no scruples, I'd have a team of ghosts operating heavy machinery to renovate this house in no time.

But patience was a virtue, I reminded myself. And I valued peace and quiet more than painted walls.

I took a lunch break, frying up eggs and bacon in the one pan I owned. I'd seen a few on the shelf in the local housewares store, but I decided to wait for a sale. There'd be one soon enough. Sales seemed to be the lifeblood of the American economy. I'd forgotten the regularity of them during my time abroad.

I felt a presence behind me and knew without looking that it was the old lady in the bubblegum pink robe, whose name I'd also deliberately avoided remembering, despite her valiant efforts to tell me. We weren't roommates, no matter how many times they drifted into the house without an invitation.

"I like my eggs poached," she said.

"Congratulations." I slid my food onto a plate and ate it at the counter.

"Why bother having a table and chairs if you're going to stand to eat?"

"Because sometimes I'm not in the mood to sit." I shoveled down the eggs and wished I'd remembered to buy hot sauce.

"You've been standing for hours. My legs are tired just watching you."

I glanced over at her. "Then stop watching me."

Her gaze traveled around the airy kitchen. "This house is awfully big for one person. Are you thinking about starting a family? How old are you, anyway?"

Bacon in hand, I pointed to the doorway. "Out."

The old woman disappeared in a huff. They'd been relatively well behaved since I spared them. It was only recently that they'd grown bolder and started encroaching on my space. At least there were only two of them. London had been so much worse.

I fell asleep after lunch and awoke to the sound of dripping water. Terrific. Now I'd have a pipe to fix before bedtime. I rolled out of bed and went in search of the source.

"It's the toilet in the downstairs half bath," Ray said, appearing at the bottom of the staircase.

"What did I tell you about house rules?"

"I found your leak, young lady. You should be thanking me."

"I'll thank you for not crossing the boundaries I set." I wasn't a fan of witches and didn't want to hire one to ward the house, but I would if it became necessary.

Ray floated to the bathroom door and pointed. "It's a simple fix. You need a new washer in the tank. They sell 'em down at Hewitt's. Ask Clark. He's real knowledgeable. Terrible poker player though. If you need money for all these jobs, he's an easy mark."

I bit my lip to suppress a smile. "I'll keep that in mind."

The old woman was on the front porch as I passed by. I tossed a triumphant glance at Ray over my shoulder. "See? This one knows how to follow the rules."

"Why is Ray allowed inside?" she demanded, folding her fuzzy pink sleeves across her chest. "I don't like these double standards."

Ignoring her, I walked across the bridge that spanned the moat and passed through the gate to where I'd parked my pickup truck, another relic of the past I bought when I moved back to the States. The truck's previous owner had taken good care of the vehicle, though, which saved me time and money.

I drove down the hill to the heart of Fairhaven. Although I'd given the town a cursory glance online, I'd been unprepared for the slice of Americana that it truly was. White picket fences. Clean streets. Charming shops that promised a superior customer experience. As a child, I'd driven through towns like Fairhaven on weekend outings with my grandfather. Pops liked to repurpose pretty much everything, which meant trawling nicer neighborhoods for trash that he then fashioned into our treasures. You wouldn't think a Navy veteran would have the kind of skills required to upcycle a wooden chair as a planter, but Pops was a man of many talents. He'd done his best to pass his skills along to me, as though he'd anticipated the struggles I'd one day face as an adult. There was nothing wrong with the way I wielded a hammer, thank you very much. I was only rusty because I hadn't needed to do any DIY during my years in London.

Hewitt's was nestled between the barber shop and a store called Recreation that seemed to cater to cyclists and other outdoor enthusiasts. Over the past six months, my trips into town consisted mainly of visits to the hardware and grocery stores. I'd checked out the housewares store twice, but that was about it. I'd successfully avoided the bakery and the coffee shop, no matter how tempting the aromas were.

I slipped into the hardware store unnoticed and listened to the sounds of friendly neighborhood chatter that included the warm weather (to be expected), the upcoming Fourth of July parade (not to be missed), and a recent supply chain issue affecting power tools (what was the world coming to?).

As I turned down the first aisle, I was intercepted by a man in a blue-and-white striped polo shirt. He looked to be in his midsixties, with salt and pepper hair and a thick beard to match. Hazel eyes inspected me from behind wire-rimmed glasses; they were curious and without judgment.

"Hello there. I'm Clark. You must be the new lady of the manor."

"Lorelei Clay. Nice to meet you." Of course he knew who I was. It was a simple process of elimination when you recognized everyone in town.

"Good to meet you, Miss Clay. I've been waiting months to meet you. Chuck seemed to draw the lucky straw the other times you've been here. Sounds like you've had your hands full from the moment you arrived, not that I'm surprised. The Castle's a huge undertaking for one person."

"Feels that way too." It didn't surprise me that locals were aware someone had bought the Castle; the development would be big news in a town of only three thousand people. Known locally as Bluebeard's Castle, the house had been built during the Gilded Age, five thousand square feet of glamour and grandeur. The original owner had been fascinated by cemeteries and more than happy to build his 'summer cottage' beside one. According to local accounts, Joseph Edgar Blue III frequently hosted seances to capitalize on his location. After World War I, his wife died, and he stopped summering in Fairhaven. After his death, the house passed to his son, Joseph Edgar Blue IV, affectionately called Quattro, whose gambling addiction sent his life into a downward spiral from which he never recovered. The house then fell into disrepair, and by the time the bank claimed it, it was a monstrous mess, with astronomical property taxes to boot. Nobody wanted it except squatters and teenagers, and it was set for demolition—until I saw it online and decided to roll the dice. Again.

Clark rubbed his hands together. "I always say I have the best job in town because I'm more likely to meet the new folks."

"Do you get many new people in Fairhaven?"

"More than you'd think. Not everybody stays until their deathbed. We lose folks to sunnier climates, mainly Florida.

You won't catch me moving to heaven's waiting room though. I prefer to spend time in all four seasons before I join the hereafter."

Despite my initial plan to grab supplies and get out quickly, I felt rooted in place as Clark continued talking.

"Fall is my personal favorite. Changing of the leaves." He paused, as though admiring them in his mind. "There's nothing prettier in the world than a giant wall of gold and red shimmering in the sunlight."

"Summer's starting to heat up," a woman said, as she maneuvered past us with a hand cart full of cleaning products.

"It's only beginning. Wait until August," Clark said. "I keep an extra roll of deodorant right here in the store." He chuckled. "That's probably TMI, right? My daughter says that means Too Much Information. For the longest time I thought it meant Tell Me Information. I'm sure you can see the problem there."

"You're rambling again, Clark," the woman called over her shoulder.

Clark cringed. "Thank you, Marcie. I'm sure Chuck didn't ramble," he said to me.

"He was very quiet," I agreed. In fact, there'd been no exchange of pleasantries at all, which had suited me fine. I preferred minimal interaction. There was something about Clark that reminded me of Pops, though, and it had been a long time since I'd encountered such a friendly older man.

"Chuck was too quiet. I had to fire him. I hated to do it, on account of I like his parents very much, but poor Chuck didn't inherit their level of competence. He seemed more interested in playing games on his phone than assisting customers." He splayed his hands. "Anyways, that's enough of my tale of woe. What are you looking for?"

"A washer for a leaky toilet."

He sucked in a breath. "Can't say I'm surprised. If you

need a plumber, we've got a few good ones in town I can recommend."

"I should be able to manage." Under Ray's watchful eye.

"Aisle 4 is where we keep plumbing supplies. Let me know if you need any help. I'm here to serve."

"Thanks, I will."

"I heard the Castle is haunted," another woman said. She had a toddler by the hand and a baby on her hip. "I was shocked when I found out somebody bought it."

"I live alone," I said simply.

I continued to aisle 4, conscious of the other customers now watching me. The friendly chatter had all but ceased; everybody seemed intent on what the newcomer was doing. I couldn't imagine anything less fascinating than browsing the plumbing aisle.

"Maybe you can all come to my house next and watch the paint dry," I murmured under my breath.

As I studied the options on the shelf, a large man rumbled down the aisle toward me. As he reached into his pocket, my body tensed and tension coiled in my stomach, ready to spring.

"You're the lady who bought the Castle, right?" He didn't wait for a response before thrusting a folded piece of paper at me. "My name's Jerry. I'm with the fire department. We host a fundraiser every year at the VFW, the evening of Fourth of July. There's a nice spread and live music. It'd be a great way to meet people."

I unfolded the paper and realized it was a flyer advertising the event. "Thanks, Jerry. I'll keep it in mind." I refolded the paper and tucked it into my purse.

"If you like brisket, you'll be in heaven," he added. "It's cooked lower and slower than any you've ever tasted."

"Sounds amazing." I turned back to the shelf and hoped that was the end of the conversation. This would be one of the differences between London and Fairhaven. In a large city, I could go all day without speaking to another living person. Unfortunately, it was the dead I couldn't avoid, and London had more than its share of lost souls. Here there were fewer dearly departed, but many more living and breathing chatterboxes who seemed to think ownership of a face was an invitation to converse.

Jerry seemed to take the hint because he exited the aisle, and I heard him say goodbye to Clark. I chose the necessary supplies and then ducked into the paint aisle for extra cans of eggshell and one additional color. I set the cans on the counter to be mixed.

Clark shot a quizzical look at the smaller can. "Red? Well, I guess the walls in your place are pretty large. You can probably get away with a color like this."

"It can work as an accent color. Do you sell hoses?"

"In the outdoor section." He nodded toward the open doorway at the back of the store. "You've got time to take a look while I mix the paint."

"Great. I'll be back." I'd been putting off the yard and the moat because the interior needed so much attention, but I'd need to get around to them sooner or later. A hose would be a good start.

In the outdoor area, an old woman leaned on a cane in front of a row of large pots. Her stark white hair was tucked haphazardly under a sunhat. She would've been my height, except for the slight hunch in her back as she leaned on her cane. When she looked at me, I saw that her eyes were a dark, luminescent blue.

"You're the lady who bought the Castle," she said.

"Lorelei Clay."

"Nice to finally meet you, Miss Clay. I'm Jessie Talbot. I've seen you in here before, but only from a distance."

"I'm looking for a hose," I told her, like she cared.

"Plenty of those in the first aisle. Be sure to buy one of

these before you leave." She used her cane to point to a wreath of dried flowers hanging on an end unit.

"Those are pretty."

"Sambucus nigra," Jessie said. "You'll see them all over town if you pay attention."

"Was there a sale or something? Why does everybody have the same one?"

She gave me a long look. "Do you know anything about flowers?"

"Not much." The garden had been my grandmother's domain. After she died, Pops and I left it to nature.

"Once upon a time, people believed this particular flower kept away witches and dark spirits."

"Once upon a time, huh?"

"Like many things, it became a tradition in town."

I touched the wreath. "Do you believe it?"

Jessie regarded me with those sharp blue eyes. "I don't just believe it. I know it."

"Have you lived here your whole life?"

"Born and raised." She relaxed her grip on the cane. "We've got a long history of strange happenings in Fairhaven. I think most folks here are used to it by now. Comes with the territory."

It hadn't occurred to me that Fairhaven could be some kind of magnet for supernatural activity. I wondered whether that was the reason I'd been drawn here, until I remembered I found the Castle online when I was still in London. Was it possible to sense supernatural energy through the interwebs, as Pops used to call the Internet?

"Do people talk openly about these strange happenings?"

"Not everybody. Some don't believe, of course. They refuse to see what's right in front of them." She used her cane to liberate the wreath from the nail and delivered it to me. "Take it. You'll thank me later."

I didn't know how to tell her the wreath was useless, so I simply carried it to the register, along with a hose.

Once I paid, Clark glanced at my purchases on the counter. "You need help carrying all this? It's a hike to the Castle from here."

"My truck is parked outside."

"Well, that makes things easier. I can help you carry everything to your truck." He didn't wait for me to accept; he simply filled a box with the paint cans and the hose and carried it toward the exit.

I hurried behind him, carrying the bag with the other supplies.

"I'm sure I'll be seeing you again soon," Clark said, placing the box in the flatbed.

"What makes you say that?"

He smiled. "Have you seen your house?"

I opened the driver's side door. "I'm taking my time. It's just me, and I don't mind the condition."

"That's a great attitude to have. Most folks these days want instant gratification. They expect a fairy godmother to fix up their money pit with the wave of a wand." His cheeks colored when he realized the insult to my house. "I'll stop rambling now. Have a good one, Miss Clay." Clark returned to the store, no doubt to chat with the remaining customers about the new owner of Bluebeard's Castle.

On the drive home, I replayed my conversation with the geriatric Jessie Talbot. I knew better than to think she was simply an elderly woman with eccentric ideas. It seemed that a deep dive into the history of Fairhaven was in order. If the town was harboring a dark and magical secret, it was one I needed to learn.

CHAPTER 2

I passed through the open gate of the Castle carrying my purchases, and noticed a large blackbird perched on the finial of the iron fence. It looked like a feathery gargoyle, warning visitors away.

"That's a big one," the pink robed ghost observed, appearing on the bridge ahead of me. "Might need a scarecrow for the cemetery."

"I think two ghosts are effective enough."

She stared at the blackbird with rounded eyes. "Birds can see us?"

"I can't say for sure. Why don't you wave your arms and do a little dance; see what it does?"

She raised her arms in the air, then suddenly dropped them to her sides. "You made that up."

I smiled. "Come into the house with me. I have a question for you."

Ray joined us on the front porch. "Am I welcome, or is the invitation only for Mrs. Pratt?"

"Please, Ray. We're dead. Call me Ingrid."

Ray shook his head. "Nope. Doesn't feel right, ma'am."

"Then call me Nana Pratt, like my grandchildren."

I shifted the box in my arms. "If you're finished with the pleasantries, can one of you open the door for me?" As much as I didn't want to encourage them to stick around, they might as well make themselves useful while they were here.

Ray glanced at the closed door. "Can I do that?"

"Focus on making contact. You have to convince yourself that you're solid."

"My wife used to say I was delusional. Maybe it'll finally come in handy." Ray stared at the door with a pinched expression.

"You don't have X-ray vision," I told him. "You're not trying to see through it. Never mind." My arms were getting sore. I set down the box and bag and opened the door.

Nana Pratt tried to lift the bag but to no avail. She gave up and let me carry it into the house.

"Did you pick up any blueberries?" she asked. "I noticed you were low."

"Stop poking around in my fridge."

"Oh, how I miss blueberries," she said.

"Strawberries were my favorite," Ray said. "With a nice dollop of ready whip." He rubbed his stomach.

"What's your question for us?" Nana Pratt asked.

I unpacked the box. "Is the library any good?" I'd been an avid user of the London Library, and I felt confident Fairhaven wouldn't be able to compete.

"Miss Hailey Jones is an excellent librarian," Nana Pratt enthused. "If you need information, she can help you."

Ray tried in vain to lift a can of paint. "If you're going there, would you mind picking up the latest James Patterson?"

"I didn't know you liked to read," Nana Pratt said.

"I didn't have anybody to check out books for me until now," Ray replied. "I wasn't sure how I felt about having a living person in my space, but I'm starting to see a few perks."

I pinned him with a hard look. "In *your* space?"

He waved a hand in the direction of the cemetery. "That's my space."

"Don't worry, Lorelei," Nana said. "We fully intend to honor your rules."

"Glad to hear it, because you know what I'm capable of if you don't." I hadn't intended to sound so harsh, but I wanted to get my point across. I couldn't afford to have nosy ghosts roaming the halls. They'd only cause trouble.

"Do you like to read?" Ray asked me.

"You know she does," Nana Pratt said accusingly. "You told me about that copy of *Pride & Prejudice* she keeps on her bedside table."

I counted to ten in my head, so I didn't banish them right here and now.

"I do like to read, Ray." I stuffed the broken-down cardboard box into the recycling bin. "And right now, I'd like to read about Fairhaven."

"Wouldn't you rather talk to the dead about it?" Nana Pratt asked.

"I'd rather talk to nobody at all," I said pointedly.

"There's a whole section in the library about Fairhaven and other local towns," Ray said.

Neither one of them mentioned strange occurrences, so I decided not to raise the issue. I'd rather read about it, and I had work to do anyway.

I took the washer into the bathroom and managed to fix the leak without input from Ray. I returned to the floorboards, careful to hold the hammer in a way that wouldn't summon the older man's spirit.

A knock on the front door startled me and I nearly whacked my thumb. *That would've delighted Ray,* I thought to myself as I answered the door. I couldn't imagine anybody in their right mind stopping by this place unannounced. I must've been too friendly in Hewitt's. Now people would mistake me for someone approachable.

A young man stood on my doorstep. Midtwenties. I classified him as reasonably attractive, albeit too young for me. By my calculations, twenty-five was still too close to the teen years.

He blinked rapidly at the sight of me. "Good afternoon, ma'am."

"Ma'am?" He was lucky I was no longer holding the hammer. "Were you expecting someone else?"

He swallowed hard. "Someone older, maybe."

I couldn't decide whether that was an acceptable answer. "Can I help you with something?"

"I don't know. I hope so, but it's going to sound kind of crazy, unless it's true. Then I guess it'll sound perfectly reasonable."

I peered at him. "Does every man in this town ramble?"

He blew out a breath and shook his wrists like he was preparing for a competition. "Sorry, I'm not doing this right. Let me start over. My name is Steven Pratt."

"What could I possibly help you with that's kind of crazy, Steven Pratt?"

His gaze flicked nervously in the direction of the cemetery. "Would you mind if I come in?"

"Oh, let him in," Nana Pratt said. "Steven's my grandson. He won't hurt you."

I glanced over to see the ghost in her fuzzy pink bathrobe hovering at the edge of the porch. The dead could manifest any outfit they wore in life. The bathrobe had likely been her favorite item.

"He wouldn't hurt an ant," she continued. "As a matter of fact, he used to walk around them on the sidewalk, so he didn't squish 'em. His grandfather called him a sissy, a word I always hated, but I knew he had a gentle spirit."

Steven followed my gaze with unease. "What are you looking at?"

"Tell him it's Nana Pratt," the old woman said.

I didn't want to say that, or anything else. Once word got out that I could talk to ghosts, I'd have people driving up the hill for a glimpse of the lunatic, and then I'd be forced to get a ward installed.

"Nothing," I said. "What brings you here, Steven?"

The old woman crossed her arms. "That's just rude. I am that boy's grandmother. He's got nobody left in this world apart from his sister, Ashley."

I shushed her.

Steven recoiled. "Sorry, I thought you wanted me to tell you why I'm here."

"I wasn't talking to you." I sighed inwardly. I knew what the next question would be.

Steven looked left to right. "Who were you talking to?"

I closed my eyes and silently cursed myself for letting her stay. No good deed went unpunished. "Nana Pratt," I told him.

To my astonishment, Steven nodded, as though this information was expected. "Does she… Does she look well?"

"She looks dead," I said truthfully. I wasn't one to sugarcoat a situation.

"Hey!" the old woman objected. "I look very good for my age and condition."

Steven swallowed again. "Like there are worms coming out of her eye sockets and such?"

"No. She looks the way you'd remember her." I sighed. "Why don't you come in, Steven? Tell me what crazy thing I can do for you."

"Can I come, too?" Nana Pratt asked. "I want to know why he's here."

I motioned for her to join us, but only because she'd asked permission first, and I had a feeling she'd press her ghostly face to the window if I refused. It would be distracting.

Steven took his time walking through the foyer. He seemed to find something new to gape at with each step. To be fair, it was a massive house that needed a lot of work to restore it to its former grandeur, not that I was planning to restore it. My goal was only to make it habitable.

"I never expected anybody to buy this place," Steven remarked. "I heard it was a pit."

We entered the kitchen, which was one of the only functional rooms in the house at present.

"And have you seen anything to change your mind?"

He snorted. "Not really." He seemed to feel bad about the insult because he added, "The moat is cool though. I don't know anybody with their own moat."

"I prefer to think of it as a lazy river." Or I would once I managed to add fresh water. Right now, the moat was problematic; the swamp-like feature drew mosquitoes during the hot and humid months. We were only at the end of June, and I was already lighting torches with citronella and cedar.

"Speaking of lazy, tell him he needs a haircut," Nana Pratt said.

"That's the style," I told her, without passing along the message.

"Any longer and he'll be parting the Red Sea."

I smiled. "I think it was more than a hairstyle responsible for that."

Steven glanced at the empty air. "Is she ragging on my hair again?"

"She is." I gestured for him to sit at the small square table. "Tea?"

"No, thank you."

"Mind if I have a cup? I'll consider this my break."

"It's your house."

I filled the kettle and set it on the stove, praying that when

I turned on the gas, the house didn't explode. There were still a lot of unknowns. "You don't seem too shocked by my ability."

"No, ma'am. It's the reason I'm here."

Interesting. There was no way he could know the full extent of my powers. "First, I'm only thirty-five, so please ditch the 'ma'am.' Second, how could you possibly know what I can do?"

He lowered his gaze and ran his fingers along the patina of the wood. "A few friends were up here one night awhile back."

"At the house?"

"Outside the cemetery. There's a wooded section where people go to drink, now that they can't drink in the Castle anymore."

I'd heard voices on occasion, but sometimes it was difficult to tell the voices of the dead from those of the living.

Steven continued to stare at the table with a fascination the boring slab of pine didn't deserve. "They said you were talking to ghosts in the cemetery."

So much for keeping my secret. "How do they know there were ghosts? Maybe I was talking to myself."

He swiveled in the chair to look at me. "They said you warned the ghosts not to enter the house without permission."

I gave Nana Pratt a pointed look. "Why is my ability the reason you're here?"

"My sister's gone missing," he blurted.

Nana Pratt gasped. "Ashley's missing?"

"I was hoping you might be able to tell me whether she…" He trailed off.

"You want to know if she's dead."

Nana Pratt clutched at her robe. "No need to be so blunt. We're talking about my sweet granddaughter."

Steven nodded slowly. "I remembered what my friends

had told me about that night in the cemetery. I didn't believe them at the time, but I thought maybe…" He inclined his head in the direction of where he assumed Nana Pratt was standing, although he was wrong. "Maybe if they were telling the truth, you'd be able to help me." He paused for a sharp intake of breath. "I told you it would sound crazy."

"Ashley isn't here," Nana Pratt said. "Tell him it's just me and Ray Bauer."

"I haven't seen your sister," I told him.

Steven's shoulders sagged as he released a breath. "Thank God. I mean, does that mean for sure she's alive?"

"Not for sure, no." But it was a good sign. A recently deceased person would be drawn to me like a bug to a zapper, unless they crossed over quickly, which often happened. It depended on the individual.

"Can you try to summon her? See if her ghost shows up?"

I poured the hot water into a cup and dropped in a teabag. "Are you picturing me in a turban with my hands clutching a scrying glass? Because that's not how I work."

"Then how do you work? Do you need an item of hers? Because I brought one." He dug into his pocket and produced a bracelet. "This is one of her favorites."

Nana Pratt drifted closer; her nose scrunched in a judgmental ball. "Is that even real gold?"

I took the proffered jewelry. "Why not rely on the police to find her?"

He lowered his head again. "The police don't want to look."

"Why not?"

"They're too busy and think it's a waste of resources."

My eyes widened at that. "Did they tell you that?"

"Not in so many words, but it was implied. Ashley's been in trouble before. They think she's run off, and she's legally an adult now, so they feel like she can do what she wants."

"But you don't think so?"

He raised his head and met my gaze. "I know my sister, ma'am." He cleared his throat, realizing his error.

"Miss Clay," I corrected him.

He waved a hand around the kitchen. "You seem like you could use help around here. If you help me find Ashley, I'm pretty good with a sander and a paint roller."

"I'm not lacking in that department," I said.

His gaze flicked to the old computer that took up half the counter space. "I'm real good with computers too. I can tell that one needs fixing."

He had me there. Technology and I weren't exactly simpatico. I'd been living without Internet service and had been relying on my phone; the coverage at the Castle was spotty on a good day.

"You've got to help him," Nana Pratt said. "These are my grandkids."

"I don't have to do anything," I snapped.

Nana Pratt's hands molded to her hips. "So help me, if you don't do what you can for my kin, I will haunt you day in and day out for the rest of your time here."

For a fleeting moment, I pictured Pops in the doorway, demanding that his granddaughter be admitted to yet another school. He would've threatened to haunt people, too, if he'd been a ghost then.

"What kind of help do you think I can offer you?" I asked. "I'm a better bet when the person is dead."

Steven flinched. "Please don't jinx it. Death is kind of a big deal."

"Only to the living."

"Stop beating around the bush and tell him you'll help," Nana Pratt demanded.

Sipping my tea, I pondered the broken computer. It would make my life easier to have it working again. Most of my money was earmarked for other necessities. The computer was so far down the list that it might as well not be on the list at all.

"Maybe you could talk to other ghosts in town," Steven suggested. "Find out if they saw anything." He tugged his earlobe. "Is that how it works? The ghosts are stuck near where they died or were buried?"

"More or less." I wasn't in the mood to discuss the details. I was still reeling from the fact that I was about to make a deal with Steven Pratt to find his sister. I blamed Nana Pratt. It wasn't too late to cast her out; I'd have to mull it over when she wasn't staring me down.

Steven's head bobbed. "Cool."

"You really don't think she left town?"

"I really don't."

"When's the last time you saw her?"

"Monk's on Friday night. I left like an hour before she did."

"I assume that's a bar."

"Well, it isn't a monastery," Nana Pratt quipped.

"What about her phone?" I asked.

"I've been calling and texting but no response, and she always kept location services turned off. The police said it would take time to get information from the mobile carrier because they need a warrant."

"And you don't think we have that kind of time," I said, more of a statement than a question.

"For red tape? Definitely not. I tried a few apps to ping the phone's location or show me the last known location, but nothing worked." Steven chewed on his lower lip. "Is anybody else with you aside from Nana?"

"Ray Bauer."

He seemed mystified by that. "Only those two?"

"Everybody else crossed over when given the chance," I explained. "Sometimes spirits need a little nudge."

"Tell him his parents weren't here," Nana Pratt said. "Remind him their ashes were scattered in the river."

I highly doubted he needed reminding about that. Still, I said, "Your parents weren't among them."

His eyes flickered with a mixture of relief and disappointment. I understood his conflicting emotions. As someone who'd lost her parents at a young age, I'd simultaneously wanted to speak to their ghosts, yet also wanted them to rest in peace. Same for my grandparents.

I looked at Steven now, potentially alone in the world, and I felt the rise of an unexpected emotion, one I didn't feel very often.

Compassion.

I inclined my head toward the computer. "You fix that monstrosity, and I'll see what I can find out about your sister."

"Really?" Steven jumped out of the chair, knocking it backward in the process. "You have no idea how much I appreciate this." He quickly bent down to straighten the chair.

"You can thank Nana Pratt. She drives a hard bargain."

Steven smiled at the refrigerator. "Thank you, Nana. I always liked you better than Granny Higgins."

"That isn't saying much," Nana Pratt said wryly.

Steven wandered over to the counter for a closer inspection of the computer. "Where'd you get this thing anyway? It looks older than Nana Pratt."

"Mind your tongue, young man," Nana said.

"I've had it for years," I said vaguely. He didn't need to know about the items I'd put in storage before I left for England. Now that we'd struck a deal, I was eager to have my house to myself again.

"I'll need to come back another time with a few tools, if that's okay."

"Just text me when you're ready. The odds are good I'll be here."

Steven couldn't seem to stop grinning as we exchanged numbers. "I'm so grateful for your help, Miss Clay. Truly. I didn't know what to expect when I came here, but you're even better than I imagined."

"Now he's just kissing your ass," Nana Pratt said with an amused shake of her head.

"You can go now," I told them.

"Thanks again," Steven said. He cast a hopeful look in my direction as he left the kitchen.

"I'll make sure he gets to his car okay. Don't need both my grandchildren going missing." Nana Pratt sailed through the wall and disappeared.

I observed the empty chair where Steven had been seated. In six months, he was the only visitor I'd had, unless you counted deliveries. I didn't mind. The whole point of choosing this house was its location. Ghostly neighbors I could handle; it was the living ones I tried to avoid. I'd mistakenly believed a big city like London would help me hide—the more people around, the less visible I'd be. It didn't quite work out that way though, not when there were so many restless spirits there. I'd spent time in many historic cities, but living in London produced a whole host of issues that I grew weary of handling. I briefly considered moving to a desolate mountain range, but I figured the Poconos were good enough. I was close to the Delaware Water Gap, which was a nice feature for someone like me who liked to kayak and hike. Solitary endeavors. Those were all I wanted, the lifestyle that reminded me of Pops.

Once I finished my cup of tea, I wandered outside with a rectangular piece of plywood, a drop cloth, a small can of paint, and a brush.

"What are you doing?" Ray asked.

"New project." I tossed the piece of wood on top of the

cloth. Dipping the brush in the can of bright red paint, I wrote 'No Trespassing.' I was tempted to write 'Trespassers Will Be Tortured,' but I didn't want to draw the attention of local law enforcement.

"You've got a big property," Ray said. "I don't think one sign's gonna do the job."

I motioned to the pile of lumber. "I have plenty of wood."

"Why not just get alligators for the moat and call it a day?"

"Now there's an idea. Thanks, Ray."

"Hey, I wasn't being serious."

Ignoring him, I crossed the small bridge that spanned the moat and hung the sign outside the gate. Nobody could say I didn't warn them.

CHAPTER 3

Painting kept my hands occupied the remainder of the day, leaving my mind free to wander. Instead of thinking about basic needs like what I wanted for dinner, I found myself thinking about Ashley. I'd been in her shoes. Adrift. Except I didn't have a brother desperate to look out for me. At her age, I didn't have anybody at all.

I rewarded myself for my manual labor with a cold IPA. I sat on the front porch with the bottle sweating next to my bare leg, observing the swath of orange that spread across the sky like an ink blot. The actual sunset was behind me to the west, a beautiful blend of pastel pinks and blues, but the more stunning view was to the east, in my opinion.

Nana Pratt materialized beside me on the porch. "Are you going to Monk's tonight to talk to the dead?"

"And the living. I'm waiting for the sun to set first."

"What does that matter? Ray and I are here all day and night."

I smirked. "No need to remind me."

I polished off the beer and carried the empty bottle inside. I worked too hard to keep the house tidy. I refused to attract ants with one careless act. I rinsed the bottle in the sink and grabbed the keys to the truck.

"Aren't you going to change first?" Nana Pratt called after me, as I exited the house.

"Who am I trying to impress?"

"Some of the men might be more open to talking if you cleaned up nicer," she suggested.

"Men who frequent a place called Monk's aren't likely to care."

I passed through the gate and climbed into the truck, thankful my ghostly companions would be unable to join me. Based on the GPS, I'd have about ten minutes of solitude before I arrived at Monk's. I didn't even play the radio. I kept the windows up to block out external noise and blasted the A/C. It was blissful.

The bar was located southeast of downtown Fairhaven, past Sawmill Creek. Its nearest neighbor was Ruby's Pet Resort, where I pictured Great Danes enjoying pedicures and bubble baths while their human companions were on vacation.

I parked my truck in the dirt parking lot. There were about a dozen cars already there. It was a shame the bar was too far from town to walk, although I bet that didn't stop a few drunks from trying on occasion.

I skirted the building, which was more of a large wooden shack that threatened to buckle under the weight of the humidity on a night like this. I wasn't ready to brave the inside, not yet.

The heat licked my bare arms as I wandered past the back door. It was propped open with steam pouring out. I hurried past, not wanting to get caught up in whatever maintenance issues the bar was having. I already had a job to do.

The woods behind the bar were dark. There wasn't much light pollution in this direction, probably because these smaller woods abutted the larger area known as Wild Acres. I scanned the trees for signs of movement. If there were ghosts in the vicinity, they'd find me. They always did.

I lingered for a good five minutes before giving up. It was time to join the land of the living. To say I was unenthusiastic was an understatement. Curse Nana and Steven Pratt and their sob story. We all had dead people; why had I let theirs influence my decision? The police were probably right. Ashley was an adult who was likely afraid of upsetting her brother, so she left without a word. Still, a deal was a deal.

I continued around the perimeter of the building before heading inside. Monk's was the quintessential dive bar. The wooden floor was covered in a thin layer of dirt and debris tracked in from patrons. I caught a whiff of pot as I approached the counter. The stools looked like they hadn't been cleaned since Nixon was president. I opted to stand.

The solo bartender was too busy serving people at the opposite end of the bar to notice me. Fine with me. It gave me a chance to get the lay of the land. I spotted plenty of supernaturals amongst the humans. From their curious expressions, they seemed to recognize me as 'other' without knowing how to classify me. Typical.

I scanned the crowd for young human men because they were the ones most likely to have noticed a pretty, young woman like Ashley the night she disappeared. My gaze landed on a target slouched against the wall. Light brown hair. Cherub face. Kind eyes. Most notably, the pint glass in his hand was nearly empty, and those kind eyes were turning into drunken slits. He might be a talker in his inebriated state.

I sidled up beside him. "What do you recommend here?"

He barely registered my presence. "Beer," he said, and laughed like a hyena.

"Do you know Ashley Pratt?"

His chin slid down toward his chest. It took me a second to recognize the movement as a nod.

"Did you see her here on Friday night?"

This nod was more perceptible.

"Did you happen to notice what time she left?"

He puckered his lips as though his mouth was doing all the thinking for him. "Eleven."

So, he could speak. I was beginning to wonder. "Was she alone?"

He tilted his head to the side, away from mine. "Yeah, she was. Tommy Mennard tried his luck but was shot down. Again."

"And what do we think of Tommy Mennard?"

"Annoying, but an okay dude. He moved on to Caitlin Roberts the second Ashley left."

I snorted. "Typical." My gaze flicked to the rest of the bar. "Is Tommy here now?"

Belching, he searched the room. "White golf shirt. Khaki shorts."

I followed his gaze to the jukebox where the white golf shirt was sandwiched between a Led Zeppelin T-shirt and a black tank top. The men of Fairhaven wouldn't be strutting the catwalk during Fashion Week anytime soon.

I patted my helper's shoulder. "Thanks. Now sober up before you go home."

"What? I'm only just getting started." He closed his eyes and slid down to sit on the floor.

I stalked toward my prey. Tommy only had an inch on me and probably weighed less, bless his white cotton shirt.

"Are you Tommy Mennard?" I asked.

He grinned like he'd won the lottery. "Yeah, I'm Tommy."

"I understand you were the last person to see Ashley Pratt before she went missing."

His grin quickly evaporated. "No, that's not true. Who told you that?"

"She was last seen at this bar talking to you."

His companions snorted with laughter. "Where'd you

stash her, Tommy?" the bald one asked. "Should we check the trunk of your car for DNA evidence?"

The other friend lit up with excitement. "Do you have one of those special lights that shows blood?"

"I'm not a cop," I said.

Tommy's brow furrowed. "Then why are you asking about Ashley?"

"Because I'm helping her brother with the search. Can we talk for two minutes?"

He glanced over his shoulder at his friends. "I'll be right back."

"She ain't a cop, Tommy. You don't need to talk to her," his bald friend said.

"I got nothing to hide." He walked with me to the far side of the room, away from the cluster of bodies.

"What did the two of you talk about that night?" I asked.

He shrugged. "Not much. Our routine is the same. I ask her out. She says no."

"If she keeps saying no, why keep asking?"

"I do it a little differently each time, like that night I offered to take her to the new seafood place."

"Because that's her favorite?"

He frowned. "No, because seafood's my favorite."

I was starting to see why Ashley wasn't interested. "Did she seem like herself that night?"

"Yeah, sure. She was worried about the police catching her drinking again, but that was nothing new."

My gaze flicked to the bartender. "They serve minors here a lot?"

"Dude, it's half their business." He tensed at his revelation, then seemed to remember I wasn't a cop. "They'd be crazy not to."

"How old are you?"

He squared his shoulders. "I've been legal for six months."

"Ashley's what—eighteen? Nineteen? Why not go for a woman your own age?"

He groaned. "You sound like my mom. She thinks I'm wasting my time on Ashley."

"Why?"

"She's been in trouble with the law a few times."

I feigned ignorance. "For what?"

"Nothing awful. Petty theft. Drinking in the woods. Smoking pot in public." The hint of a smile formed. "I like a woman who doesn't bow to societal norms. It's hot."

"There's a difference between wearing a nose ring and breaking the law."

"Says you." Tommy hesitated. "The thing is, I really like Ashley. I don't want anything bad to happen to her."

"Did you see her talk to anybody else before she left?"

"No, she said she had to leave and walked straight out the door."

"Did she say why?"

Tommy shook his head. "Didn't see the point in asking. She would've lied anyway."

Tommy Mennard seemed harmless, although I could understand Ashley's aversion to him. Pestering her for a date, no matter how many ways he tried, wasn't going to win him one.

"Do you think she's ... alive?" he whispered.

"We hope so." No need to tell him about my ghostly radar if he wasn't already aware.

He jabbed a thumb over his shoulder. "Can I get back to my friends now? It's Doug's turn to buy a round, and he always cheaps out if he can get away with it."

"Go for it."

He returned to his friends, and I strode to the counter to talk to the bartender. It wouldn't be easy with this crowd, but if there was someone else here with information about Ashley, the bartender was the best person to tell me.

He tossed a beverage napkin on the counter. "What can I get you?"

"Information. I'm looking into the disappearance of Ashley Pratt."

His brow furrowed. "You a cop?"

"No, but I have professional experience tracking people down." That much was true.

He continued serving drinks while he spoke to me. The movements were second nature to him. "I saw her shoot down Tommy Mennard for the hundredth time, and then she left."

"No arguments? No drama?"

He shook his head and passed a beer to an outstretched hand. "Nope. Nothing special about that night at all. I know Ashley's been in trouble but never in here."

"How often does she come here?"

He licked his lips, and I could tell he was debating the level of honesty he wanted to offer.

"I know she's under twenty-one," I continued. "I don't care about that."

His shoulders relaxed. "She's one of my regulars. Then again, pretty much everybody here right now is a regular."

"Thanks." I left money on the counter for his time. As I turned to leave, my shoulder slammed into the shoulder of a middle-aged brunette. Fire sparked in her brown eyes, and her upper lip curled into a snarl. There was no mistaking her shifter vibe.

"Watch where you're going," she growled. I smelled stale beer on her breath.

Her friend grabbed her arm in an effort to tug her away. "Relax, Anna. It was an accident."

Anna did not relax. The touch of our shoulders must've alerted her to my otherness, and her body stiffened in response.

I didn't want an incident. I quickly held up my hands, apologetic. "It won't happen again."

Anna didn't seem so sure. She cut a glance at Tommy Mennard. "I saw you talking to Tommy. Are you some kind of succubus? Have you come here to suck our boys dry?"

I cringed. "I'm not here to suck anybody. Promise."

Her gaze raked over me, seemingly unconvinced. "I don't like you. You smell weird."

"That's rude," her friend hissed.

Anna was drunk and itching for a fight. I got the sense that no matter how I responded, she'd still throw a punch to end the conversation.

I glanced at the can of Bud Light in her hand. "If you're planning to crush a beer can as a display of strength, at least rinse it out first so it can be recycled. There's the environment to think of."

Anna's companion stifled a laugh; my aggressor's nostrils flared in response. "Outside. Now."

The companion paled as she realized the evening was about to take a violent turn. She tugged on her friend's shirt. "Anna, just leave it. She's nobody."

"All the more reason I need to teach this nobody a lesson, so she doesn't mistake herself for somebody in this town." Anna's hostile gaze lingered on me. She was scared, but too drunk to understand why. To be fair, even if she were sober, she wouldn't know unless I told her.

I debated the best way to handle the situation. I didn't see a way of diffusing it without some sort of physical altercation. On the other hand, I didn't want to draw attention to myself.

"Just the two of us," I said.

Anna smiled. "No witnesses. Sounds good to me."

Her friend whimpered. "Can we not do this, please?"

Anna thrust her beer can at her companion. "Stay here and have another beer waiting for me. I'll be two minutes."

To me, she said, "You might want to ask for a napkin to wipe off the blood."

"It's fine. I've never been a fan of this shirt anyway."

I followed her outside and around the corner to where the dumpster squatted between the building and a cluster of oak trees.

She flexed her fingers, preparing to curl them into fists. I didn't give her the chance. My hand shot out and gripped her shoulder. I *pushed* into her mind and was surprised by the number of options. In the interest of time, I chose the most prevalent one.

A younger version of Anna skipped rope outside a trailer. A wind chime tinkled as a gust of wind blew through the row of homes. Young Anna stopped jumping and lowered the rope.

I waited, curious to see where this was going. Creepy stalker? Vampire attack?

The earth shifted, causing the trailer to tilt. Anna turned as a giant hole opened beneath the trailer and swallowed it whole. A scream tore from Anna's throat. She dropped the rope and started to run. The ground seemed to chase her as chasm after chasm appeared behind her, claiming everything in its path. The girl's face appeared strained, and I realized she was trying to shift in order to run faster. For whatever reason, she couldn't. All part of the nightmare.

I released my hold on her shoulder. "Sinkhole, huh? I guess they are pretty scary."

Anna staggered backward, gaping at me with wild eyes. "What did you do to me?"

"Nothing you haven't done to yourself. How many times have you had that nightmare?"

Her face scrunched together as though she was resisting physical pain. "I've had it off and on since I was seven."

"Is it based on a real event?"

She shook her head.

"Consider yourself lucky then. Go back to your friend. Tell her you kicked my ass."

Anna's head snapped back in surprise. "Why would I do that?"

"Because you're proud and drunk, and because I don't want anybody to know about this."

She continued to cower in the shadow of the dumpster. "Then why do it?"

"Because I need you to leave me alone, and now you will. I moved here to live a quiet life in as much solitude as possible."

"Then you should've gone deeper into the mountains."

"Makes it harder to buy paint." And almond butter. I was a big fan of almond butter. "I need you to promise me you won't tell anyone about this. If you do, I can make that nightmare come alive any time I want. It would make life unbearable for you. Do you understand?"

She offered a gruff nod. "How can you do that?"

"You left me no choice."

"No, I mean *how*? What kind of power is that?"

"One I didn't ask for," I said simply, and walked away.

I almost made it to my truck. Almost.

I spotted the red lights and knew somebody inside had called the cops, probably expecting a bloodbath. Anna had a reputation, no doubt.

The SUV pulled alongside me. The woman behind the wheel gave me a hard look. She was midthirties; the ends of her choppy brown hair stuck out from beneath a pageboy hat. Two crescent moons cradled her eyes; she looked sleep deprived and deeply unhappy about it.

"Are you the one fighting with Anna Dupree?"

"Do I look like I'm fighting with anyone?"

She inspected me, searching for signs of injury. "What's your name?"

"Lorelei Clay."

My gaze dropped to the badge on her shirt. Chief Garcia. I didn't expect the police chief to look like an extra from Newsies.

"Enjoy your night at Monk's, Miss Clay?"

"It was an experience."

Her gaze shifted to my truck. "Have you had anything to drink?"

"No, Chief."

"Then why come?"

I decided to come clean. Maybe it would garner me points. "I was here to talk to people about a missing girl. Ashley Pratt."

The chief emitted a small sigh. "Did Steven Pratt hire himself a detective?" She paused. "No, he doesn't have the money for that," she said, more to herself. "Anything he makes goes to paying the mortgage on their house."

"I'm not a detective."

The chief cut the engine. "Why don't we sit down over there and talk for a few minutes?" She nodded toward the unmatched pieces of outdoor furniture that looked like they'd been salvaged from the dump. Pops would've at least given them a fresh coat of paint.

I wasn't thrilled by this development, but if I could establish myself as a helpful, law-abiding citizen, it might keep me off their radar.

We wandered over to the outdoor area; she sat in the lawn chair, and I took the end of a bench.

"Lorelei Clay," she murmured. "I know that name. You bought the big pile of blue stones."

"That I did."

She continued to gaze at me. "Huh."

"Huh, what?"

"I thought you'd look older and a little crazier."

"I left my bulging eyeballs at home, but I can wear them next time if it helps."

Chief Garcia smiled. "Tell me why you're searching for Ashley Pratt."

"Her brother asked for my help. He said she's been in trouble before, and that the police don't seem interested in finding her."

Closing her eyes, the police chief pinched the bridge of her nose. "It isn't that we don't want to find her. It's that we believe she doesn't want to be found."

"What makes you think that?"

"Because we think she used the money she stole from the register at the pharmacy where she'd been working part-time to fund her exit."

Ah.

"Maybe she used the money for other necessities," I countered. "It sounds like they're cash strapped."

The chief nodded. "Steven's struggled to keep the family home ever since their parents died. He works two jobs."

"Yet you think Ashley used the money she stole to leave town without telling him?" It seemed to me she'd feel inclined to help ease her brother's burden. Then again, maybe running away would accomplish that goal.

"Ashley has had a lot of issues since their parents died."

"Can you blame her? The loss of your parents is a traumatic event, especially when you're young." I knew that firsthand.

The chief gazed up at the sky. It was too cloudy to see the moon or any stars. "Why did Steven come to you?" The twitch of her right eye gave her away; she'd heard the rumors about me. I was curious to know exactly what she'd heard.

"He thought if his sister was dead, that I might be able to contact her ghost." The only way to control a story is to get ahead of it, and I was, apparently, woefully behind.

She didn't miss a beat. "I guess you didn't, or you wouldn't be here asking questions."

"If Ashley is dead, it didn't happen in this area."

The chief rubbed the spot between her eyebrows. I had a feeling she did that often enough to leave a dent. "He really is worried, isn't he?"

"He is." I tilted my head. "You seem very accepting of my claim."

The chief sighed. "If you live in Fairhaven long enough, you hear a lot of farfetched stories. Some of them even turn out to be true."

"Have you ever met anyone who can communicate with spirits?"

"Only the medium my sister took me to see in Brooklyn."

"Were they any good?"

Chief Garcia grunted at the memory. "She told me that my first love had passed and that he wanted me to know I'd always hold a special place in his heart."

"That's horrible. And he was still alive?"

"No, my first love was Meghan Parker. She's very much alive and well, and still hates my guts to this day because I accidentally outed her to her family."

"Ouch."

"No kidding." She slotted her fingers together across her lap. "Can any of your ghost buddies confirm whether Ashley is alive or dead?"

"Ghosts aren't omniscient. That isn't how it works."

Her eyes sharpened. "Then how *does* it work?"

I saw it then, the flicker of distrust. It didn't take a psychic to figure out that she thought I might be connected to Ashley's disappearance.

"Where'd you come from, Miss Clay? I heard London, but you don't have an accent."

The small-town grapevine was no joke. "You heard correctly. I grew up here though."

The chief's eyes widened. "In Fairhaven?"

"No, Bucks County."

"What did you do for work in London?"

"I ran my own agency tracking down lost heirs."

"Any money in that?"

"Depended on the case. I earned a percentage of the assets in return."

She leaned back against the chair and assessed me. "So, you were sort of an investigator. Any police training?"

"None at all."

"If I look you up online, I'll find your agency information?"

"It was by word-of-mouth only." Usually, the word of a ghost telling me to find their long-lost son, or third cousin twice removed, or whatever the situation.

"You weren't licensed?"

"I'm not a big fan of bureaucracy, and I *might* have been living and working on a tourist visa."

The chief smiled at that. "Is that why you left? You got caught?"

"Yes," I lied. "Anyway, Steven seems desperate for help, and I'm desperate to have a working computer, which he agreed to fix. I think it's a fair deal."

The chief tipped her head back ponderously. "What if you're the reason Ashley is missing and you're trying to find out how much people know?"

"For what purpose?"

"So, you can cover your tracks? Skip town? Plenty of options to choose from. You have to admit, the house you purchased is awfully big for one person. You could easily hide a dozen girls in there without anybody being the wiser."

"And do what with them?" I held up a hand. "Wait. Don't answer that." I was glad I was getting this conversation out of the way now. Sooner or later, they would've shown up on my doorstep. Best to control the timing and their impression of me. "You're welcome to search the house. Just be mindful of the mess. It's basically one big construction zone."

Chief Garcia regarded me in silence for a moment. Finally, she seemed to reach a decision. "I'll be honest, I'm glad Steven has help. We're short staffed at the moment. We lost one of our officers about a month ago."

"She relocated?"

"She died." Her voice was flat.

"I'm sorry to hear that."

"If you see any ghosts about five feet tall with brown curly hair, that's probably Officer Lindley."

"I'll keep that in mind. Can I ask what happened to her?"

"There've been a spate of animal attacks in the woods. That's what Officer Lindley had been investigating when she was killed."

That wasn't the answer I expected. "She was killed by wild animals?"

"We found her blood in the woods, as though she'd put up a fight." The chief stopped abruptly; although her face didn't betray her, I sensed the emotions rising beneath the surface. She was trying to keep them from cresting in the presence of a stranger.

"Her blood," I repeated. "Not her body?"

The chief cleared her throat. "No body. We assume..." She trailed off, but I didn't need to ask for clarification. I knew exactly what they assumed.

"Aren't you concerned that Ashley might've met the same fate?"

"It's unlikely. We haven't found evidence of her blood anywhere, and the last place she was seen was right here, which you obviously know. It's a short ride home from here."

"And the woods are right there." I gestured to the area behind Monk's. "Nobody knows which way she went."

"What did the folks inside tell you?"

"I spoke to the bartender and Tommy Mennard."

She snorted. "He asked her out again that night, huh?"

I nodded. "They said she left around eleven."

"Alone?"

"Yes. No drama."

The chief arched an eyebrow. "For someone without police training, you seem to know what you're doing."

"I'm tracking down a missing relative, which is basically what I did in London."

"True. What are you doing for work here?"

"Right now, I'm pouring all my energy into the house to make it habitable."

"I can understand that. It's a mammoth job. Why not hire professionals?"

"Money." And privacy. Always privacy.

"I know what you paid for that heap. It's public record. Why spend so much, knowing what it would take to restore it, if money was an issue?"

She was digging now. Unfortunately for her, I had no interest in divulging more than I had. "It seemed like the right place at the right time, so I went for it."

"I bet you could've found plenty of old houses to restore in England."

"The Castle is the one that spoke to me."

This got her attention. "You can speak to houses too?"

I laughed. "I meant metaphorically." The moment the building appeared on my phone screen during a property search, I knew I had to have it.

"Do you still have family in Bucks County?"

"Not anymore. I lived there with my grandfather until he died. Then it was the foster care system for a couple years." I had no doubt Chief Garcia would be running a background check on me the second she returned to her office. I was mildly surprised she hadn't already.

Her expression softened. "I'm sorry."

I shrugged. "I survived." My experience as a foster kid was probably the reason I ended up choosing to hunt down lost heirs in London. I wanted people to find their remaining family members, to connect even after death. My special skills helped my success rate, of course. The last case I handled resulted in an enormous payout, the kind of money that allowed me to buy the Castle and live in solitude until I figured out my next steps. I knew the money wouldn't last forever, though, so I was careful about my expenditures. The faster I spent my savings, the faster I'd have to rejoin humanity. I was happier alone.

"I'm starting to understand your desire to help Steven. Their parents died three years ago. Flash flood." Frowning, she paused, as though remembering the horrific event. "Steven's fairly responsible, but Ashley was at that age where trauma hits extra hard, you know?"

I knew.

"Bar fights. Petty theft. Nothing major, but all attention seeking."

"Hard to get attention if you're not around to reap the benefits."

"My guess is she took a bus to New York City, and she'll turn up in another week with a few wild stories and grateful to be alive."

Something in her expression gave me pause. "You're worried."

Her expression was grim. "I worry about everything, Miss Clay. The environment. Human rights. The rise of neo-Nazism. I used to worry about the ozone layer, but that seems to have been resolved, thankfully." She pushed herself to her feet. "It was good to put a face to the name. If you learn anything of interest, I hope you'll pass it along."

"I will."

I waited until she got into her SUV and drove away to return to my truck. No need for a police escort home. I glanced in my rearview mirror for any sign of Anna, although I assumed the werewolf was long gone by now.

For six months I managed to evade the locals. Six months of just me and my toolkit and the occasional ghostly intrusion. Sighing with regret, I backed out of the parking spot and turned onto the road.

All good things must come to an end.

CHAPTER 4

The next morning was hot and sticky, the kind of humidity I didn't expect until August. My first clue was the dampness of the T-shirt and shorts I'd slept in. I'd have to figure out how to cool the house sooner rather than later. An air conditioner wasn't feasible for a house this massive. I could buy single units for the rooms I occupied the most, basically the kitchen and the master bedroom. Of course, even single units didn't come cheap, and I'd spent most of my savings to buy this fortress of solitude.

I washed my face with cold water and meandered downstairs to the kitchen for tea. There were just enough yogurt and blueberries for one more breakfast. A trip to the store was in order. I should've done it yesterday when I was in town. It wasn't that downtown was far; it was that it was full of people, and I'd had more than my fair share of social interaction yesterday. Two trips into Fairhaven in as many days was pushing me out of my comfort zone. Pretty soon people would recognize me on sight; I didn't need that, although they seemed able to identify me anyway as the one person in town they didn't already know. And I was already headed to the library. Might as well keep driving east afterward.

The Fairhaven Public Library was situated at the quiet end of Main Street, away from the Delaware River and midway up the hill toward the Castle. The nearest neighbor was a bank that looked old enough to have been robbed when the getaway car was a stagecoach.

The parking lot bordered on empty. Perfect. I didn't want anyone to overhear my questions, and I had a feeling the mere sight of me would draw eavesdroppers, depending on the rumor they might've heard.

The door opened automatically, and I approached the counter where a stout, middle-aged woman was busy typing on a computer. She wore her dark brown hair in tight curls.

I cleared my throat, prompting her to look up.

She pushed her cobalt blue glasses back to the bridge of her nose. "Oh, gosh. I'm so sorry. I was in the zone." She offered me a cheerful smile. "Does that ever happen to you? Where you're so fully in your head that it's like the rest of the world doesn't exist?" She knocked on the side of her head.

"Sounds good to me," I admitted. "Are you Hailey Jones?"

"I am. You must be Lorelei Clay. I've got your library card ready for you." She ducked behind the counter and popped up, holding a laminated card.

"How did you…? I didn't apply for one yet."

"Oh, I always prepare one in advance for anybody new. Any excuse to laminate."

I accepted the card. She'd even spelled my name correctly, which I appreciated. "I need the latest James Patterson," I said, temporarily thrown off guard.

Her eyebrows knitted together. "Okay, I wouldn't have guessed that about you, but I can tell you where to find it."

My gaze drifted to the stacks behind her. "I'd also like to see books with information on the town's history."

Her face lit up like the Fourth of July. "You're a history buff?"

I forced a smile. "It only seems right to learn about my new hometown."

She clapped her hands. "I'm so thrilled. Yes, I can absolutely help you. Right this way." She shimmied out from behind the counter and started walking toward the stacks on the left side of the library. Her long skirt swished around her ankles as she walked. "You have no idea how happy this makes me. History is so important, but people don't realize the crucial role it plays in the present." Her voice faded as she disappeared down an aisle ahead of me.

I caught up with her in the middle of the aisle where she'd already extracted an armful of books from the shelf.

"These are a good start." She thrust the pile into my arms. "Is it true you're looking for Ashley Pratt?"

I maintained a neutral expression. "What have you heard?"

"That Steven Pratt asked you for help in exchange for him fixing your antique computer."

I burst into laughter. "That is surprisingly accurate."

Hailey squared her broad shoulders. "I'm the librarian. It's important to get information right." She cast a furtive gaze around us and lowered her voice. "Is it also true you can see ghosts?"

"Yes," I whispered. There was no point in lying to Hailey about that part. I'd inadvertently given up that particular secret, and there was no easy way to put the lid back on the coffin.

Her brown eyes sparkled. "My grandpa had the Sight, but he couldn't see ghosts. Gosh, I was so envious of him. He had access to an entire world most of us can't see." Her sigh was laden with regret.

It seemed that Hailey was in the believer camp, along with Jessie Talbot. "Well, you can see them," I said. "You just don't recognize them as anything other than human."

She dropped her voice even lower. "I would beg him to

tell me which people were werewolves, but he didn't like to talk about it. He'd say, "Ignorance is bliss for a reason, Hailey," and then change the subject." She smiled. "I work in a library, so you can imagine how the 'ignorance is bliss' line landed with me."

"Is that why you have the wreath on the library door?" I'd noticed it on my way in, but the sight of it only registered now.

Her brown eyes turned solemn. "I don't know that it's effective, but the library has never had a bad incident, so the wreath stays. My mother considered it a good luck charm."

"Has anywhere had a bad incident?"

"I guess it depends on what you think really happened," she replied vaguely.

The librarian seemed fairly plugged in, so I decided to probe her about Ashley. "Have you heard any rumors about Ashley's disappearance?"

Her face clouded over. "A couple."

"Does one involve her hopping on a bus to New York City?"

She nodded. "Another one involves human trafficking."

That was a new one. "Chief Garcia didn't mention that theory."

"You might want to talk to Otto Visconti. He lives in that big house over on Walden Lane." Hailey dropped her voice. "Some people find him a bit strange, but he donates a truckload of books to the library every year, so we're big fans."

"You think he might know something about human trafficking in Fairhaven?"

"Maybe not, but he has the kind of connections who might."

Connections was an interesting choice of words. I wanted to ask more questions, but a man appeared at the end of the aisle, looking agitated.

"Hailey, I can't get the checkout machine to work. It won't scan my card."

"I'll be there in two seconds, Ronald." She smiled at me. "Technology is both a blessing and a curse."

I didn't disagree.

I chose a book entitled *A Complete History of Fairhaven*, curious to see whether it lived up to its name and left the rest on the table. "I'll check this one out." It was about two inches thick; there had to be some useful information in it.

Hailey lit up as though she'd closed a sale. "Great choice. I'll get your new James Patterson, and you'll be all set. I hope to see more of you, Miss Clay. The library is always thrilled to add a new reader to its roster."

The house on Walden Lane was easy to find. Twin columns stretched from the front porch all the way to the rooftop. The second and third floor each boasted its own balcony that spanned the width of the house. Black shutters contrasted nicely with chalky white paint. The double doors were painted a glossy red that reminded me of cheap lipstick.

I rang the bell and waited. A woman finally answered; either her face had succumbed to gravity, or she was deeply unhappy. Possibly both. She wore a white collared shirt, a black skirt, and black flats.

"Hello. I'm here to see Mr. Visconti."

The woman's dark eyebrows lifted, and I got the distinct impression Mr. Visconti didn't entertain visitors very often. I liked him already. "Is he expecting you?"

"No." I decided to keep my response simple. If she wanted more information, she'd have to dig for it.

The woman shifted awkwardly, appearing uncertain how to proceed. "I'll need to check that he's available. Wait right here. Please," she added, almost as an afterthought.

She closed the door and left me standing on the front

porch. I took the opportunity to survey the area. Otto's house was the only one on this block. If I had to guess, I'd say the house had been built before the road. I pictured a horse-drawn carriage waiting out front for its owner to alight, quite possibly the same owner I was about to meet.

"Right this way, miss," the woman said. I'd been so preoccupied by my surroundings, I hadn't heard the door reopen.

I passed through the red lips and let the house swallow me whole. I stepped into a large foyer with a sweeping staircase to a room at the far end of the first floor. The interior was a blend of styles; Otto seemed reluctant to settle on one. The wallpaper consisted of a green and gold interlocking floral motif, and the artwork included a statue of the goddess Diana that featured only her head and torso, as well as a modern painting that seemed straight out of a child's coloring book. If I stood in the foyer too long, I'd walk away with a migraine.

The woman escorted me to an open doorway and scurried away, as though desperate not to be privy to the conversation. In her haste, she forgot to announce me, not that she'd bothered to ask my name.

I entered the darkened study where I heard the soft click of a metronome. In the dim light, I saw Otto Visconti hunched over a piano. Even seated, I could tell he was little more than five feet. Five-two if I was being generous.

He lifted his head at the sound of my approaching footsteps. "It isn't often I receive strangers. With whom am I having the pleasure?"

"My name is Lorelei Clay. I'm new in town, the remorseful buyer of the Castle."

His body stiffened. Otto was a vampire; he didn't need the gift of Sight to sense I was more than a friendly new neighbor. "What brings you here of all places, Miss Clay?"

"I was looking for a change."

"I can't identify you."

"I told you my name."

A whisper of a smile passed his lips. "So you did. I do not fear you, you know, whatever you are." His trembling hands betrayed him. He quickly dropped them to his sides and balled them into fists.

"Glad to hear it." I needed to put him at ease, or I wouldn't get any information out of him. "What do you like to play? *Witch's Lament*? A little *Agony*?"

His simple huff was packed with derision. "Screw Sondheim. I loathe *Into the Woods*. It's banal and pedestrian, everything a musical shouldn't be."

"How do you feel about jazz?" I asked. "I think vampires are genetically wired to like jazz."

"I'd rather electrocute myself in a puddle of my own piss."

"Jazz makes me twitchy," I said, "so I can understand that."

"It makes me want to rip the sax from the musician's hands and beat him over the head with it."

Alrighty then. "You're not in danger of winning any congeniality awards, are you, Mr. Visconti?"

Otto snorted. "Certainly not. No one's ever accused me of fawning. I live alone for a reason."

"Your staff doesn't live with you?"

"No. There's a day shift and a night shift." He paused. "Is this visit to alert my kind that there's a new sheriff in town, so to speak?"

"My visit to you isn't any kind of statement. I'm looking for a missing young woman by the name of Ashley Pratt."

He struck one of the keys. "I don't recognize the name. You won't find her here."

"I wasn't expecting to find her chained in your basement." Although now that I'd met him, it wouldn't surprise me to find *someone* chained there. "Have you heard anything about missing young women? There's a human trafficking theory flying around."

"Why is someone of your obvious stature interested in a missing human?"

"I made a deal with her brother."

Otto tilted his head toward me. "Why not compel me to answer?"

"I can't perform magic, Mr. Visconti." He was probing for more information about me. The truth was I had no direct control over the undead, only influence, and without knowing Otto's age, I wasn't sure I'd be successful. The older the vampire, the more resistant he was to my power. It didn't stop them from being uneasy around me though. Like Otto, they oftentimes sensed *something* about me, even if they didn't know exactly what.

Otto seemed satisfied by my response. "How about I make you a deal then? If you can tell me how many beats per minute this is," he said, motioning to the metronome, "I'll answer your questions."

"Eighty-six," I said. "I also have perfect pitch in case you were wondering." I didn't get many opportunities to boast about that particular skill.

His lips peeled back, showing off a set of polished fangs. "Sing for me. I'd love to hear it."

"I'm only here for one purpose, and it isn't a solo."

Otto tilted his head. "You used to play."

"Not anymore."

"You miss it. I can hear it in your voice."

"The information, Otto. We made a deal."

Otto nodded. "And a Visconti always keeps his word."

"I assume the rumors of human trafficking involves vampires. Know anything about that?"

"Nonsense. We have systems in place to keep the peace. There would be no need for us to resort to criminal activity."

"Would you be in the loop if they were?" Otto was old but he was also a recluse. It was possible younger vampires were breaking the rules behind his back.

He stared at me with milky white eyes. "I thought your interest was in one missing girl. I don't see what importance any other girls have. They are, by your account, still alive."

"I think it's obvious. If vampires are trafficking people, Ashley could be one of them."

Gently, he stroked a key. "If there are vampires committing such heinous acts, I have no knowledge of it. I no longer touch human blood. Everybody who knows me knows that."

"Do you mind me asking why?"

Otto snorted. "You ask as though no one's told you the story."

In fact, no one had, but I played along nonetheless. "Stories take on a life of their own. I'm interested in your version of events."

Otto directed his absent gaze at the wall ahead. "I'll tell you mine if you tell me yours." The vampire seemed to have forgotten his earlier unease.

"I moved here to forget mine."

He smiled at that. "Bourbon helps too." He played a scale. "I was an arrogant and unpleasant vampire once upon a time who paid a price for my behavior."

Once upon a time? More like here and now. "And you've been off human blood ever since?"

"I have no choice. The curse prevents me from drinking human blood. One drop and I'll perish. The blindness was an unexpected consequence."

"Of the curse?"

"Of me trying to stop the curse from happening." Otto paused. "The one who cursed me no longer lives, in case you're wondering."

"Sounds like quite an ordeal." I wasn't expecting that kind of story. It wouldn't surprise me to learn he'd become a recluse because the other vampires had shunned him— other vampires who were trafficking humans for their blood.

"I have a question for you now," he continued. "Why is it that women named Anya are always whores?"

I was beginning to understand why Otto didn't entertain visitors. "I don't know anyone named Anya," I said. Then again, I didn't know a lot of anybody, which suited me fine.

"Consider yourself truly blessed."

I was losing patience with the vampire. "Is this a riddle, Mr. Visconti?"

The intensity of his playing increased. "No, simply a slap at my ex, who's been getting off with yet another vampire if the rumors are to be believed."

"She's human?"

"Very much so. Has a thing for vampires, I discovered too late. She was married to a human when I met her, so I assumed I was her first. Her husband is a car salesman who sold me a vintage Jaguar. I collect antique cars, you see. I later learned he screwed me on the car while she screwed me. I wasn't the first vampire to ride her either." He shook his head and said, "I should've known she was trouble."

I was uncomfortable hearing the sordid details of Otto's personal life. I barely acknowledged my own.

"You collect cars you can't drive?" I asked.

Otto's head snapped to attention. "Is that so different from collecting dolls that you don't play with? Or coins that you don't spend?"

"I don't collect anything, so I couldn't say. Why are you telling me this story about your ex, Mr. Visconti?"

"Because I'd like to offer you a deal. I would be willing to make inquiries about trafficking and your missing human if you'd be willing to make her suffer."

Curiosity got the better of me. "Suffer how?"

"However you choose. A lovely scar on her face would do. She's rather vain, and it would keep her out of the spotlight. Attention has always been a drug to her. I would relish cutting off her supply. Honestly, I don't know how she draws us in. My hands told me she isn't even very attractive."

"Then why get involved with her?" I asked.

"Looks don't matter as much to someone like me." Plink went the key.

"Because you're blind?"

"How insensitive of you, Miss Clay. Because I'm horizontally challenged. A short stature as a male vampire is an undesirable trait."

"Which is why you were unpleasant and arrogant."

"Indeed, to mask my perceived inadequacy. Yet another reason I mastered the piano. It's a rare talent to be able to play with hands this size." He wiggled his short, stubby fingers.

"A Napoleon Complex."

"A myth," he replied. "Napoleon was at least average height. It was simply an inept attempt to convert foreign measurements."

"What makes you think I can cause your ex any suffering?"

"I sense power in you. Whatever it is, use it to cause her pain."

It seemed that, despite the curse on him, somebody still hadn't learned his karmic lesson. "I'm sure there's a random psycho you could employ who could give you a similar outcome. Or maybe a witch with a spell to make her undesirable to vampires."

Otto turned back to the piano keys. "I do not engage with witches."

"I try my best to avoid them too," I admitted.

"Have you spoken to the police chief? For a human, Elena Garcia is more than competent."

That sounded like high praise coming from the curmudgeonly vampire. "I've spoken to her. At this point, I think local supernaturals are my best bet."

He rubbed the pads of his fingers over the keys. "We are

rather like modern gods, aren't we? Meddling in the lives of humans. Changing their course."

"You're a vampire, Mr. Visconti, not a god. There's a difference."

"Is there?" The question was clearly meant to be rhetorical.

"I won't get involved with your ex," I said calmly. "If that's the only way you're willing to help, then I'll leave now. Thank you for your time."

I turned toward the door, making sure my footsteps were loud enough to hear. I made it three steps before I got the result I wanted.

"Wait," Otto said. "I may be able to help you."

I turned back slowly. "And what would you like in return?"

"To learn the reason for your move to Fairhaven. I love a good scandal, even better when it's someone else's."

"There's no scandal, Mr. Visconti."

"Very well then. Visit me once a week for a month and come bearing gossip. I'd like to hear it from a newcomer's perspective. That's my price."

It came as no surprise that Otto Visconti was painfully lonely.

"Fine," I said, sinking as much reluctance into the word as I could muster. "But only if you play the piano when I visit. Nothing overly dramatic."

"Like Rachmaninoff," we said in unison.

Otto's fangs gleamed in the dim light. "Oh, I like you, Miss Clay. I very much hope you stay."

CHAPTER 5

I didn't need a ward to tell me something was wrong. I sensed it as soon as I crossed the bridge over the moat. The fact that my front door was now hanging off its hinges was another fat clue.

Nana Pratt wasted no time in intercepting me; her hands fluttered nervously. "I tried to stop them, but they ignored me."

I squeezed through the narrow gap left by the crooked door and crossed the threshold to see beams of wood strewn across the floor. "You're a ghost, Nana. They don't know you're there.

"They found out the hard way," Ray chimed in. "We followed your advice on convincing ourselves we're still solid and went full poltergeist."

Ah. "So, this mess is actually from you, not the intruder?"

"The door was their handiwork," Nana Pratt sniffed. "I don't have that kind of power."

"Not yet," Ray corrected her. "I think if we practice, we could get there in no time." He seemed pleased with this development.

"How many were there?"

"One," Nana replied. "I used 'they' because I couldn't tell if they were male or female. They wore a hood."

A sharp cry from outside interrupted the conversation.

Nana Pratt raised a finger. "Oh, I forgot to mention, there's some sort of kerfuffle happening in the cemetery."

"Describe the kerfuffle."

"A disagreement," Nana said. "Possibly a violent one."

"Can kerfuffles be violent in nature?" It was more of a rhetorical question. "Is it related to the break-in?"

"I don't think so," Ray said. "The intruder left alone about an hour ago, and these two showed up about ten minutes ago."

"At first they were having what seemed like a very pleasant conversation," Nana chimed in. "They were both smiling, until the meeting took a turn."

I crept out the front door and along the side of the house to the cemetery. I felt the presence of the ghosts behind me.

Another cry of pain erupted from between the headstones. One man had his steel-toed boot pressed down on another man's chest. His eyes were outlined in black, and his lashes were cartoon thick. His red leather pants and black feather boa seemed out of place for both the town and the weather. He swung the boa around his neck with aplomb.

"Do you know them?" I whispered.

Nana nodded. "I've seen them before—you wouldn't forget the young man with the fluffy scarf. I think the man on the ground is Alan Wentworth."

I glanced at her. "Do we like Alan Wentworth?"

She hesitated. "I have no opinion of him. We attended church together for years, until I stopped going."

"Because you died?" I asked.

"Because I stopped believing."

I inched closer and watched from my hidden position behind a headstone as the fashionable man held up a tarot card in front of Wentworth's face. I squinted for a better view. The Death card.

"Not that," Wentworth pleaded, squirming beneath the heavy boot. "Anything but that."

The card holder rolled his eyes. "It doesn't mean literal death, silly. Don't you know anything?"

His hand shaking, Wentworth pointed. "Death is written right across the top, and there's a skeleton riding a horse and holding a scythe. What else can it mean?"

The card holder paused to draw an annoyed breath. He struck me as the type of guy often annoyed about something. "In our business, Mr. Wentworth, it's the change card."

Wentworth appeared to relax. "I'm not afraid of change. I wouldn't have been able to build a multi-million-dollar business if I were."

"I'm glad to hear it, because your life is about to take an unexpected turn." Bending over, he tucked the card in Wentworth's pocket and gave it a firm pat for good measure.

Wentworth immediately started to choke. White foam bubbled from the corners of his mouth. He reached for the other man's leg, who gracefully sidestepped Wentworth's chubby fingers. He rolled onto his side and vomited. "You said it wasn't bad," he rasped.

The well-dressed man crouched to address him. "I didn't say it wasn't bad; I just said you wouldn't die." His joints cracked as he resumed an upright position. "Not today, anyway."

"What's happening?" Nana Pratt asked in horror.

"I'll tell you in a minute." I emerged from my hiding spot. "Nice boots," I said. Beginning an awkward conversation with a compliment seemed like the safest move.

The fashionista smiled, showing off years of pricey orthodontia. "Thanks. Kicking might've been required, and there's no better pair of shoes to wear under the circumstances." He extended a long, lean leg to show off his boot.

I didn't disagree. "Who's your victim?"

The smile morphed into a scowl. "He's not a victim. He's a perpetrator known to the actual victims he swindled as Alan Michael Wentworth."

Wentworth was too busy moaning and clutching his stomach to defend himself.

"What are you doing to him?" I asked.

"Teaching him a valuable lesson that will hopefully encourage a change in his criminal behavior."

"Hence the Death card."

He smiled again, and I caught another glimpse of his perfect teeth. "Tarot cards are my preferred weapons."

I'd never heard of anybody using the cards as weapons. "You're a mage."

"I am, indeed," he said with a dramatic flip of his boa. "These cards are more powerful than you know. I'm a god, holding the entire universe in my hands. I alter reality with the touch of a card."

"What a coincidence. I can alter reality with a touch, too."

He spread his arms wide. "As if a human weapon could injure me. I invite you to try."

I cocked my head. "Who said anything about a human weapon?"

That seemed to humble him. He dropped his arms to his side with a disappointed huff. "Who are you?"

"We'll get to that." I had more questions of my own, but first I needed to make sure Wentworth didn't die, mainly because I didn't want to have to evict another ghost from my property.

"Then let's move this along because I have an appointment with my optometrist in…" He checked his digital watch. "Twenty minutes."

I observed Wentworth as he attempted to crawl away, his belly dragging across the grass that was damp from humidity. How far did he think he could get?

"Do you really think this guy is going to stop cheating people because you made him vomit in a cemetery?"

The mage toyed with the fringe on his boa. "It sends a certain message."

I couldn't bear to watch this play out. "This is pathetic. Can you stop the spell?"

The mage heaved a weary sigh. He patted his pockets and produced another card. In a few long strides, he reached Wentworth. He leaned over and wiped Wentworth's drool with the second card before sliding it into the man's shirt pocket.

Wentworth grew still and quiet. I thought the mage might have killed him instead, until the portly man sprang to his feet with surprising agility and took off toward the gate.

The mage stared after him in admiration. "Wow. I wouldn't have pegged him as a sprinter. Did you see how fast his legs moved? He'll have shin splints tomorrow, for sure." The mage returned his focus to me. "Now, tell me who you are." He sounded more curious than annoyed.

"A Good Samaritan." Not that I wanted that title. I would prefer to be in a ratty T-shirt with a paint roller in one hand and a bottle of beer in the other. I wanted music playing in the background, the kind with a beat that would keep me motivated. Repetition tended to bore me, most likely because it was out of my comfort zone, one of the downsides of a disorganized childhood.

The mage seemed delighted by my answer. "Ah, my natural nemesis."

"Because?"

"I'm an assassin." He pulled another card from his pocket; thankfully this one was a business card. He handed it to me with a dramatic flick of his wrist.

"Gunther Saxon," I read aloud. An assassin named Gunther. Well, it wasn't like his mother knew his future career path when she gave birth to him.

"Friends call me Gun," he said.

Much more appropriate. I held out my hand. "Lorelei Clay."

He shook it with a light grip.

"It doesn't actually say you're an assassin on the card."

"That's what the logo is for." He pointed to the picture of two crossed swords on the card. "Don't worry, I won't hold this little snafu against you, Lorelei Clay."

"That's very generous."

"But if it happens again, I won't be as easygoing." The glint in his eye assured me that his words were genuine.

"If you're an assassin, why didn't you kill him?"

"Because it's prohibited."

I squinted at him. "Sort of defeats the purpose of calling yourself an assassin if you feel compelled not to break the law."

He rolled his eyes, and I was tempted to tell him if he did it one more time, they'd freeze that way.

"No," he said. "I mean it's prohibited in Fairhaven. That's the deal. We can live here and hold our meetings here, but only if we agree not to conduct business inside the town border."

"You hold meetings?"

He flung the end of his boa around his neck. "We're a guild. Of course, we hold meetings. You're looking at the secretary. I take the official notes. Very copious ones, I'm told."

"Congratulations."

"Hey, it wasn't an easy win. My rival is very popular, although he buys his suits at Men's Wearhouse, a crime of fashion not so easily forgiven."

"I don't understand. If you're not allowed to conduct business here, then why were you torturing Wentworth?"

He scoffed. "If I were torturing him, I would've broken his

bones." He paused. "Not all of them, only a few of the smaller ones."

I remained skeptical of his claim. "And the rules are okay with that?"

"The rules don't say anything about breaking a man's will."

"Even if your interaction with him qualifies as business?"

"Technically, it doesn't. Nobody paid me to intimidate him. He swindled money from a friend, so it's arguably a favor."

I'd have to take his word for it. "Who allows you to live and meet here?"

The assassin suddenly found the cracks on the exterior wall of Bluebeard's Castle fascinating.

"Oh, their identity is a secret? Then how would I report a violation if I witnessed one?"

His gaze swung back to me so quickly, I worried his neck would snap. "Except you didn't witness one," he said firmly. "I told you; this was a favor."

"I'm talking hypothetically."

His shoulders sagged; he seemed resigned to telling me more than he wanted to. "There's a regulatory body."

It was like pulling fangs from a vampire, which I'd done. More than once. "And who's in charge of the regulatory body?"

"Kane Sullivan. He's not our boss, though," Gunther added quickly. "He only makes sure we operate under the rules and punishes us if we don't."

"What's the punishment?"

"Don't know. Nobody's ever crossed the line."

Interesting. "And all the assassins are fine and dandy with oversight by someone you didn't choose?"

"Nobody says no to Mr. Sullivan," he said with an air of reverence.

I looked in the direction of the gate, through which Wentworth had fled. "Why not let the police handle your buddy Wentworth?"

"The local cops are down one these days, and they're busy with bigger problems. Plus, I wanted to help my friend. He didn't deserve to lose his savings."

"Oh, so you're one of those honorable assassins." I was well aware of my mocking tone.

My attitude didn't seem to ruffle the mage's feathers. "I care about my friend. There's nothing wrong with that." His face grew pinched. "This is what's wrong with the world today. You don't want guys like me to feel anything. I'm supposed to be this big, bad killing machine." He adjusted his feather boa. "Well, guess what? I have emotions, and I'm not ashamed of them." He pressed a fist to his chest, over his heart, and I noticed his fingernails were painted a deep plum color.

"Then you don't carve a line in a wooden panel every time you kill someone?"

His hand dropped to his side. "Oh, I totally keep a record of my kills, but I feel conflicted about it."

"I see." An idea occurred to me. "Do you ever get local jobs that involve lesser crimes like kidnapping?"

He leaned his hip against one of the taller headstones. "I'm not aware of any kidnappings. That's too likely to result in complications."

"How many members of the guild are there?"

"Twenty."

"And where do they meet?"

He looked at me askance. "You think I'm going to reveal the location of our secret meetings to a stranger?"

"It's a small town. There can't be many places that can fit twenty big personalities." Then it dawned on me. "Where can I find this Kane Sullivan?"

Gunther's eyes narrowed. "Aren't you a clever one?"

"My former teachers would disagree."

He cracked a smile. "Mine too. School isn't for everyone, you know? It caters to the middling middle."

I folded my arms. "You might as well tell me. In a town as small as this one, it'll be easy enough to find out."

He plucked a loose thread on the boa. "The Devil's Playground."

"And that's where you hold your meetings." It wasn't a question.

Gunther pressed his lips together. "The drinks are good, and sometimes he'll throw in entertainment."

"Jugglers?"

He snorted. "Sure. Let's go with that." His gaze swept the area, as though checking for eavesdroppers before continuing. "Mr. Sullivan is an enigma to most of us. To most of the town, really. He seems to have been here forever, but nobody remembers when he showed up or knows much about him."

"And yet this mysterious figure is in charge of your guild."

Gunther pulled a face. "I already told you; he isn't in charge. We govern ourselves, and he provides oversight."

"Do you trust him?"

Gunther laughed. "You can't trust anybody in this town. That's why all the factions are so insular."

"Are the assassins all like you?"

"Sweetie, nobody's like me."

"I mean are they all mages?" I paused. "Magi?"

He appeared thoughtful. "I guess our guild is the one group with a bit of diversity. Everybody else tends to stick to their own kind. Wolves, vamps, fae, humans. We all live in the same town, but you'd never know it."

"Why is that?"

"Beats me. That's how it was when I moved here, and it hasn't changed since."

The humans I understood. They had no knowledge of the supernaturals. They probably believed they were simply steering clear of 'freaks' or 'weirdos.' Werewolves and vampires made sense too—the two groups were natural enemies. It was possible they set the tone for the rest of the species.

"When's your next meeting?"

He waved a dismissive hand, revealing a silver bracelet with dangling charms. "No way. I've said enough as it is. I'm no snitch."

"I'm not interested in taking down the guild. I'm looking into a kidnapping." Although I wasn't sure it was necessary to question every assassin in Fairhaven, I was sorely tempted. In a small town like this one, one out of twenty assassins was bound to know *something* about the disappearance of a local woman.

"You weren't kidding about the Good Samaritan part."

"Have you heard anything about vampires trafficking young human women in this area?"

"I haven't seen any evidence of it. The vampires here tend to behave themselves."

"Would you do anything about it if you did know?"

Gunther considered the question. "Only if I had a connection to the girl." His eyes skimmed me. "Not all of us can be Good Samaritans."

"This is a peaceful cemetery," I said. "In future, I ask that you carry out your empty threats elsewhere."

He gave me an appraising look. "Wait a minute. You're not *that* good. You're the lady who bought that mountain of rubble." He flicked a dainty plum fingernail behind me.

"It isn't rubble. It's actually in decent shape." I eyed him closely. "You didn't happen to venture inside before your buddy got here, did you?"

His whole face brightened. "No, but I'd love a tour. I haven't been inside since…" He puckered his lips, seeming to think better of his statement. "Never mind. It was years ago. I'm sure the bloodstains have washed away by now."

"I appreciate your enthusiasm, but I'm in the middle of multiple projects, so a tour isn't in the cards. No pun intended."

Gunther bowed. "It was nice to meet you, Lorelei Clay. I'm sure we'll see each other again, hopefully, under more pleasant circumstances next time."

I had no doubt. Gunther Saxon would be hard to miss.

I returned inside the house to deal with the second disruption of the day.

"I'm glad he didn't try to hurt you," Nana Pratt said, trailing behind me.

"He would've been sorry if he had." I was focused on the break-in now, all thoughts of Gunther Saxon pushed to the back of my mind. "Did the intruder take anything?"

"Not that I noticed," Nana said. "They seemed to be looking for something. They went straight to your computer."

I laughed. "They won't find anything there."

"They quickly drew the same conclusion. After that, they didn't seem to know where to look. They scanned the countertops and then went upstairs to your bedroom."

I shivered. My bedroom was my innermost sanctuary. Knowing it had been violated by a stranger unsettled me.

"They didn't stay long. I think once the intruder realized you didn't have what they wanted, they left," Nana said.

I really didn't want to ward the property. I disliked dealing with witches, not to mention the fact that I was short on cash at the moment. The witches I'd crossed paths with in the past had been partial to hefty monetary incentives.

"Thanks for looking out for me," I told the ghosts.

"That's what neighbors do for each other," she said simply.

"That hasn't been my experience, but I appreciate the sentiment." In London, my upstairs neighbors blared loud music at all hours, and my downstairs neighbors let their pet iguana, Buster, loose at least once a week. Buster seemed determined to take up residence in my flat because that's where he inevitably ended up.

I retraced the intruder's steps based on Nana and Ray's account, but I didn't see anything amiss.

"Could've been looking for drugs," Ray said.

"Or something they stashed here before you bought the place," Nana added.

"I thought the Castle had been empty for years," I said, although I knew that wasn't strictly true from others' comments.

"Oh, it was, but people crashed here off and on. If I wanted to hide something, I would've chosen this place too," Ray said.

"Why come back six months later?"

"Maybe they wanted to come sooner, but they couldn't," Nana offered. "Could be a convict coming back for their booty."

Ray looked at her. "The convict is a pirate?"

"I don't suppose you two paid much attention to the squatters and whoever else stayed here."

"They weren't as interesting as you," Nana said simply.

"I'm flattered." I closed the drawer to the bedside table that had been left open by the intruder. As this piece of furniture was my purchase from a thrift store, I highly doubted the intruder was looking for an item they'd stashed here.

"Did that young man really use a card to make Alan sick?" Nana Pratt asked. "Or was it some sort of magic trick?"

"It was magic, but it wasn't a trick. Were you aware of supernatural activity here when you were alive?"

Nana blinked. "You mean ghosts and such? Heavens no."

"Not just ghosts."

Ray shook his head. "There was the odd person here and there, but I didn't think much of it. Live and let live was my motto."

"I heard whispers of strange people, but I figured they were only stories," Nana said. "I never believed any of them."

I had a feeling most of the humans in Fairhaven shared their attitude.

Ray looked at me with a blank expression. "So, what are you?"

I offered a wan smile. "I'm a woman who can talk to the dead."

"Does that make you one of the supernaturals?" Nana Pratt asked.

"The answer is complicated. That's all you need to know."

That was all anybody here needed to know.

CHAPTER 6

Given the time of day, I expected the Devil's Playground to be closed. The bouncer who intercepted me at the door suggested otherwise. The bald, muscled vampire looked at me with a dollop of derision and a dash of fearful uncertainty, which meant he wasn't as dumb as he looked. He pushed his hand into his fist and flexed his arm muscles, as though that might dissuade me from wanting to enter. Sorry, pal. You'd have to do much better than a gun show.

"I'm here to see Kane Sullivan," I said.

"We're outside of normal business hours. Is Mr. Sullivan expecting you?" His voice rumbled like a well-performing muffler.

"No." I didn't offer any further details, which unsettled the bouncer. I had no doubt he was used to more accommodating patrons.

His dark eyes glimmered with hesitation. "What's your name?"

"Lorelei Clay."

He tapped his earpiece, which I hadn't noticed before. "Lorelei Clay is here to see Mr. Sullivan."

It took another minute, but the vampire begrudgingly let me pass. The move from the entrance to the lounge was like passing into another realm. If Monk's specialty was Bud Light in a can, then the Devil's Playground specialty was surely champagne cocktail in a flute. The establishment was far swankier and more upscale than I expected for a lounge in the middle of nowhere. For a bar that was operating outside of regular business hours, there were a surprising number of bodies circulating the room; they far exceeded the number of cars in the parking lot.

I noted signs for three smaller rooms in addition to the main lounge area, as well as a large hot tub on a balcony overhead. The hot tub was currently occupied by two silhouettes. I couldn't determine their species from this angle and judging by their close proximity to each other, I didn't want to investigate any further.

Red and black were the signature colors. How original. To be fair, one could hardly design the Devil's Playground interior in pastel pink and purple.

The pulsating music was set at a reasonable volume, probably due to the early hour. A raised platform with a piano suggested performances by a live band. I briefly wondered whether Otto ever ventured here. It seemed like his style.

There were enough patrons that no one seemed to notice me. It gave me a chance to study the clientele. I counted more vampires than any other species. Unlike the movies, real vampires could function in daylight, although they were more powerful at night. These vampires were clearly more interested in having a good time than flexing their abilities. They wore more formal attire, like beaded dresses and collared shirts, and I suddenly felt underdressed in my black tank top and dark denim shorts.

As I maneuvered past a seating area comprised entirely of crushed red velvet furniture, I became acutely aware of someone watching me. I glanced over at the bar and locked eyes with the bartender. He was every bit as decked out as the patrons in a red collared shirt and charcoal vest that hugged his sculpted torso. I could see why Sullivan had hired him. With dark blond hair that covered his head in soft waves and cheek bones carved by stone masons, he possessed the kind of otherworldly beauty that would make anyone believe they'd died and gone to heaven, even if they were standing in the center of the Devil's Playground.

He arched a pale eyebrow, an invitation.

His scent hit me as I slipped between the stools to stand at the counter. It was earthier than I would've guessed. I associated musk and sandalwood with werewolves. There was also a hint of pine, which offset the musk. Maybe the crowd had rubbed off on him, except the current clientele favored supernaturals with more fangs than fur.

"I'm looking for Kane Sullivan," I said.

Whisky-colored eyes examined me with interest. "Congratulations, Ms. Clay. Your journey has reached an end." He extended a hand across the counter. When I didn't take it, he slipped it in his pocket. His movements were elegant, refined. Now that I was directly in front of him, I felt ridiculous for thinking he was the bartender; he radiated power.

"Is there somewhere we can talk in private?"

Despite his angelic appearance, there was something decidedly *not* innocent about him. It was his full mouth, the way his lips curved ever so slightly, hinting at all that his mouth was capable of. He promised you both mind-blowing sex and a cooked breakfast afterward.

"No one will overhear us if that's your preference," he said. His voice matched his eyes, whisky smooth.

I smiled. "There are about twenty vampires behind me that would beg to differ."

He waved his hand and silence engulfed us. It was as though we were insects and he'd overturned a glass to cover us in a protective bubble.

He leaned forward provocatively. "Do go on, Ms. Clay."

"You're a demon."

"You were expecting something else?"

I hadn't given it much thought until now. "I need you to keep your assassins off my lawn."

The invisible dome shook with his laughter. "That's one I haven't heard before. What happened? A skirmish between them? They have a tendency to fight and make up within a matter of minutes. It's the temperament, I think. They're a feisty bunch."

He talked about the assassins like they were children on a playground. "One of them was threatening a human on my property."

"And what property is that?"

"Bluebeard's Castle. Technically, the cemetery next to it."

His expression remained unchanged. "You must like a project if you're willing to tackle that one. You might have an easier time trying to change a man."

The joke caught me off guard, and I snorted inelegantly. "Are you volunteering?"

He made a face. "I said a man, Ms. Clay. Demons are quite a different species."

I didn't disagree.

"I'll have a word with the guild about minding boundaries." He wiped his hands on his vest. "Where are my manners? Here you are in the finest cocktail lounge in the region, and I've yet to offer you a drink."

"What do you recommend?"

"I mix a fabulous old-fashioned."

Of course he did.

"No, wait. Let me think." His gaze raked over me, pausing to linger on the swell of my breasts beneath the thin fabric of the tank top. "I'm afraid I don't serve craft beer, but I can offer you a gin and tonic."

I felt vaguely insulted. "Seltzer water with lime is fine."

"As you wish."

Music flooded my ears as the invisible dome dissipated. He filled a glass with seltzer water and affixed the wedge of lime to the edge of the glass.

He slid the glass across the counter to me. "Now it's my turn."

"For what?"

"I understand you're looking for a missing woman."

I brought the glass to my lips and drank. "Who told you that?"

"I believe half the town is talking about it, while the other half listens." He wore a vaguely amused smile.

"Know anything about her?"

"The girl? No. I'm afraid not. She's never visited my fine establishment."

"How can you be sure?"

His cufflinks caught the light as he gestured toward the entrance. "Because I'm aware of every soul who steps through those doors. We're very discerning about our clientele, as you can imagine."

As I set my glass on the counter, my gaze snagged on a creature lurking in the shadows. I did a double take. Even in the dim light I saw the cat's shining mismatched eyes and striking two-colored face, with orange on the left and black on the right.

Kane followed my gaze to the corner. "That's Sunny. She's a chimera."

"Is she friendly?"

"That depends, and you don't wish to find out the hard way."

"She bites?"

"Worse. She breathes fire."

"She's very pretty."

"She knows it too. She's an arrogant little thing."

I couldn't help but smile. "Aren't all cats?"

Sunny seemed to know we were talking about her. She stood on all fours and walked away with her nose in the air.

"You don't worry about her getting crushed by an unruly crowd?" I asked.

"Sunny can take care of herself."

I toyed with my glass. "What kind of clientele do you get here?"

"All sorts. These are locals, but we serve people from the city. They like to drive to this area and stay at B & Bs on the weekends."

"Weekends must be intense for you."

"Those are certainly our busiest nights of the week, but I leave the labor to my staff."

I motioned to my glass. "You served me."

"I serve only those I wish to serve. One of the perks of ownership." He poured himself a glass of Yamazaki. How appropriate.

"What's your stake in this missing girl business?" he asked.

"Why is everyone so interested in my motivation?"

"Because it doesn't fit what I know about you."

My fingers tightened around the glass. "And what do you presume to know about me, Mr. Sullivan? We only just met."

He seemed to realize his mistake and projected an apologetic air. "Only that you bought a fortress on the outskirts of town where you live alone. You've been here for six months but barely venture out and haven't received visitors. Those actions don't strike me as someone who's enthusiastic about getting involved in the lives of locals."

My jaw hardened. "It isn't a fortress."

"I wager it will be when you're done with it."

His comment rankled me. "And where do you live? I can't imagine it's somewhere cramped and cozy."

"I live right here, as a matter of fact." He glanced toward a door at the far end of the lounge area.

"Doesn't your work life bleed into your personal one?"

He shrugged. "Business, pleasure. They're the same to me."

"Why this place?" I pressed. "Is it the energy? Do you feed off it?"

He wagged a finger at me. "Naughty Ms. Clay. You won't wheedle anything more out of me. If we're playing strip poker, that means we *both* take off our clothes."

I tugged on the edge of my tank top. "I'm not wearing extra layers."

"Maybe not, but your armor is quite apparent." His expression grew curious. "Why would Chief Garcia allow you to involve yourself in an official investigation?"

"Because there isn't an official investigation. Plus, she seems overwhelmed. She's down one cop, and there seems to be a rabid animal on the loose terrorizing livestock."

"Ah, yes. I've heard about that."

"What have you heard?"

His full lips curved ever so slightly. "That there seems to be a rabid animal on the loose terrorizing livestock." He swirled the liquid in his glass. "It's good that you're involved, I think. Chief Garcia is capable enough, but she's hampered by her…" His eyebrows drew together.

"Her humanity?"

He allowed himself a small smile. "More or less."

I decided to open the door a little wider. "What's been your experience with the humans in town? Do they know about supernaturals?"

"Many do, thanks to generations of experience. I even believe the remainder do on a subconscious level, but they find it difficult to reconcile with the known world."

"What's the attraction for supernaturals? Why Fairhaven?" I was curious if he had an opinion, or perhaps even direct knowledge.

His whisky eyes focused on me. "What brought you here?"

"A desire for solitude and a fresh start."

He laughed lightly. "How's that working out for you?"

"Too soon to tell. What brought you here?"

"Retirement."

I inclined my head toward the lounge area. "You don't seem retired."

"The clientele here suits me." There was something about the way he said it that gave me pause.

"Are you sure you're not an incubus?"

He laughed. "Quite, but I'm terribly flattered that you would mistake me for someone with such incredible sexual energy."

In that moment, I would've been perfectly fine if the floor rose up and swallowed me whole. "What kind of demon are you then?"

He leaned across the counter so that his full lips were whisper-close to my ear. "I'll tell you mine if you tell me yours."

I shifted to the right to escape the tickle of his breath on my bare skin. "I have nothing to tell."

"You're more than a ghost whisperer, I'd wager." He seemed to stare straight into the depths of my soul; part of me wondered whether he could.

"You heard about that?"

He chuckled. "Of course. You'll find I'm somewhat of a collector of secrets. Stay here long enough, and I'll have yours eventually."

"Is that a threat?"

"Not at all. I don't use them as blackmail or to expose anyone. They're purely for my own enjoyment."

"You have a strange way of amusing yourself. Is that why you oversee the Assassins Guild? Shits and giggles?"

He sipped his whisky. "Ah, I see."

"See what?"

"There's no joy in your life."

"Excuse me? I have joy."

He set down his glass. "Very well then. Tell me what amuses you. What makes you laugh when no one's around?"

I struggled to come up with an answer. "This is your way of getting personal information out of me."

"I'm going to go out on a limb and say what brings you joy is a secret even from you."

A woman straddled the stool next to me. Her lips parted sightly, revealing two sharp fangs. "I've been waiting for you to notice me, Kane, but you've been too preoccupied," she complained.

"The usual, Vanessa?"

The vampire flung her thick hair over her shoulder. "I'd like to change it up tonight. Surprise me."

"Oh, I like your attitude." He snapped his fingers, and a bartender seemed to appear out of nowhere. It seemed Kane wasn't joking about only serving those he deemed worthy. Tough break, Vanessa.

The actual bartender was bare chested underneath a black leather vest and matching shorts. I tried to not think about the level of chafing. Even with the air-conditioner running at full blast, the outfit seemed ill-suited to summer weather.

As she awaited her drink, Vanessa eyed me curiously. "Are you from the city?"

"This is Lorelei Clay. She's new in town," Kane said smoothly.

Vanessa continued to stare at me, appearing slightly unnerved. "Are you a witch?"

"Definitely not," I said.

Vanessa's fangs pressed into her lower lip. "Then why do I feel like I want to run?"

"I imagine it's that her beauty intimidates you," Kane interjected.

Vanessa studied me. "No, that's not it."

Kane suppressed an amused smile.

The bartender set a highball glass on a coaster in front of Vanessa, and the vampire squealed. "Cole, it's like you can read my mind." She held up the glass to salute Kane. "This is why I come back as often as I do. You always know how to please a woman."

Kane pressed his lips together. "I'll let that statement stand."

Vanessa brought the glass to her red lips and took a delicate sip. "It doesn't seem to be the usual crowd. Is there an event happening somewhere else?"

"It's my understanding that business has been quiet across the board. Something's keeping patrons away, though I have no idea what."

"Well, it certainly isn't the eye candy." She winked at him.

Kane bowed. "You flatter me, Vanessa."

The vampire turned her focus back to me. "If you're looking for a place to frequent, this is the one you want. Everyone who's anyone like us hangs out here."

"Like us?" I repeated.

"Supernaturals." Her gaze flicked over me. "I don't know what you are, but whatever it is, it isn't strictly human." She sipped again. "I don't get it. You don't look like much. Why do I feel this sense of dread?"

"Maybe it isn't me."

She swiveled on her stool and surveyed the room. "I recognize most everyone in here. It has to be you."

Vanessa was awfully stubborn for a vampire professing to be wary of me. I needed her to drop the subject, or she was going to manifest her unfortunate destiny.

Kane seemed to sense the building tension because he said, "Vanessa, darling, why don't you spend time with Hollis? She looks exceptionally lonely over there by the piano."

Vanessa's lips curved into a seductive smile. "I adore Hollis. She tastes like cherries and brandy." With a drink in hand, Vanessa slid off the stool and sauntered toward Hollis.

"Whatever you are will be impossible for you to hide here, Ms. Clay," Kane said. "You'll need to practice your answers more carefully."

"I don't know what you mean."

He looked at me intently. "I think you do."

"It's Miss Clay," I said. I wasn't sure why I suddenly felt the need to correct him, but I did.

His expression lightened. "Ah, here's someone you should meet. If it isn't my favorite vampire."

Another vampire hurdled over top of the counter and landed beside Kane with the grace of a panther. Her dark hair was pulled tight in a high ponytail, accentuating her heart-shaped face. Wide-set eyes were framed by thick lashes.

"Josephine Banks, meet Lorelei Clay, the proud owner of Bluebeard's Castle." Kane's gaze skated to me. "Josie is my head of security."

Two sharp fangs gleamed in the atmospheric lighting. "I was wondering who would be crazy enough to buy that money pit."

"Or wealthy enough," Kane added.

Josie examined my outfit. "Well, it clearly isn't money."

Ouch. I mean, she wasn't wrong but still.

"What brings you in here?" Josie asked. "This doesn't strike me as your kind of place."

Another ouch in quick succession. Josie didn't hold her punches, which seemed apt for the head of security.

"You've packed a lot of assumptions into that statement," I said.

"It's part of the job—reading people quickly, determining their threat level." She poured herself a shot of tequila.

"And what level am I?"

She downed the tequila and smacked her lips in satisfaction. "Right now? I'd say a three."

"Why right now?" I asked.

"Because you have power, but you don't like to use it, so it would take a lot to set you off. I can't tell what kind of power though." Her tongue flicked across her cherry-red lips. "One little sip will tell me."

She started forward, but Kane's arm shot out to block her before she could make it across the counter.

Josie pouted. "She didn't even flinch."

"Not my first enthusiastic vampire," I said, remaining perfectly still.

Josie raised the bottle of tequila. "Shot?"

"Not now, thanks." I figured I'd lob my next question while I had the head of security in front of me. "Have you heard anything about vampires trafficking human girls?"

"In Fairhaven?" Josie asked. "No way."

"Why not here?"

"Because Kane wouldn't allow it." She angled her head toward him.

"It would be bad for business," Kane explained.

"I'm glad you cleared that up. Wouldn't want to mistake you for a demon with a conscience."

"If there were vampires trafficking anybody within a twenty-mile radius of this town, I'd know about it," Josie said, with a touch of arrogance.

"How about the animal attacks?" I asked.

"I know about the dead cop," she said. "Too bad. I liked Lindley."

"You knew her?"

Josie nodded. "Can't be head of security of a place like this without knowing the local police."

"Do you think she really died from an animal attack?" I asked.

Josie seemed to choose her words carefully. "I think she was likely killed by whatever's been killing the livestock."

It was a reasonable theory. "Would it be possible to interview your friendly neighborhood assassins during their next guild meeting?"

Kane started to choke, prompting raucous laughter from Josie. "Check out the balls on you," she said, giving me an admiring glance.

"I'm afraid that won't be possible," Kane said, "but I'm more than willing to conduct my own inquiry. If I learn anything, I'll let you know."

I could tell that was as far as I could push him. I had one more question though. "If I were in the market for a ward, would you have a recommendation?"

Kane and Josie exchanged glances. "Bridger?" he asked.

Josie mulled it over. "I'm not sure they're taking small jobs. They won that jackpot last year, remember?"

I laughed. "They won the lottery?"

"I don't think it was a particularly large sum, but it made the news," Kane said. "It would be worth asking. Penelope Bridger is one of the older and more talented witches in the area."

"Thanks."

He waved me off when I opened my purse to pay for the seltzer water. "I look forward to seeing you again soon, Miss Clay. It's been an absolute pleasure."

I wasn't so sure about that, but it wasn't entirely *un*pleasant either.

"Take my card before you go." He plucked a business card from his pocket and placed it in front of me on the counter.

"Why?"

"In case you discover any more assassins on your lawn, of course."

I tucked the card into my purse.

Noise broke out behind us, and Josie swung into action, vaulting over the counter toward the brawl.

"Cole, tell Darby there's a patient headed her way," Kane called over his shoulder.

"You keep medical personnel on the payroll?" I asked.

"Darby is one of the fae, and yes, I keep her on staff. As I'm sure you know, their blood is a universal healer." He frowned at the ruckus behind me; it seemed Josie only managed to continue the brawl. "I'd advise you to leave now, Miss Clay. Things are about to get messy."

I exited the building, conscious of the looks of interest I was receiving from the clientele on my way out. Apparently, I was more interesting than the fight. The humidity clung to my skin as I walked to my truck. Kane Sullivan was a powerful demon with secrets; that much was certain. Naturally, he was the authority figure in charge of a supernatural assassins guild. If he was harboring a dark secret, such as a nasty habit of kidnapping young women, I wanted to know sooner rather than later. Whether he'd correctly identified me was another matter. I could be any number of beings; there was no reason to believe his supernatural radar was as impressive as the rest of him.

I shook my head to clear my thoughts of Kane. He'd probably slipped something in my drink to make me think highly of him. Arrogant prick.

Apart from the occasional chirp, the town seemed unnaturally quiet as I drove home with the windows of the truck rolled down. It seemed as though every resident in Fairhaven was slumbering, like the part in Sleeping Beauty when the fairies cast a sleeping spell over the kingdom. It was incredibly peaceful; so peaceful, in fact, that I lingered on my front porch to enjoy it a little longer before I went to bed.

One thing that bothered me more than the owner of the Devil's Playground was the number of paranormal patrons. I had no idea that Fairhaven was a magnet for others, or I never would've decided to put down roots here. It seemed strange that I'd chosen a small town that was some kind of supernatural epicenter. It couldn't be a coincidence. If it was more than Bluebeard's Castle that had lured me here, I needed to know.

Noisy crickets disrupted my thoughts as I climbed into bed. *The Complete History of Fairhaven* beckoned me from my bedside table, but I was too tired to read. I closed my eyes and let them sing me to sleep.

CHAPTER 7

The witch's house wasn't what I expected. It wasn't as though I anticipated a gingerbread cottage or anything like that; I'd known enough witches not to be fooled by stories. Still, a white farmhouse with outbuildings and chicken coops wasn't on my supernatural bingo card.

I passed through the gate of the white picket fence and walked along the stone path to the porch. The front door was open, leaving only a screen door in view. I heard the click before I saw the shotgun. Me being me, I continued to the door as though I'd heard nothing at all.

"What do you want?" the voice behind the gun demanded. A smoker's voice. Interesting. I'd never known a witch to touch cigarettes.

"My name is Lorelei Clay. I understand there's someone here who might be able to help me with a problem." I arrived on the wraparound porch. With a swing and cheerful potted plants, the porch was more welcoming than she was.

"We all got problems. Why would I help you?"

I wasn't keen on talking to the barrel of a shotgun, so I

decided to cut to the chase. "Since when do witches need guns?"

"When we want to dissuade trespassers."

"Why not use a ward?" If she couldn't create one, better to know now so I could be on my merry way and find someone who could.

"I do use a ward. That's how I knew you were here. Mine is set for detection, not prevention. I own a farm. I deal with the public. It might arouse suspicion if people can't set foot on the property without blowing up."

She had a point. I couldn't set up a ward that prevented the police chief from passing through the gate to the Castle. Chief Garcia was human; she'd assume there were, in fact, criminal activities taking place beyond the iron fence.

"I need a ward around my property like yours, one that alerts me to trespassers," I explained. "I had a break-in recently, and I don't want a repeat performance."

She pressed her face closer to the screen door. Her skin was riddled with liver spots and dark circles nested under her eyes. Corkscrew curls the color of bullets rained down around her face. "You look human. Who told you I could make you a ward?"

I didn't bother to correct her assumption. "Kane Sullivan."

The witch's eyes widened, and she lowered the shotgun. "You know the demon?"

"We're recently acquainted. When I told him I needed a ward, he suggested I pay you a visit. You are Penelope Bridger, aren't you?"

"I am. Come in, Lorelei Clay." The witch opened the door and gave me an appraising look as I entered.

She put on the safety before she nestled the shotgun in a set of hooks on the wall and motioned for me to follow her. "Why the need for a ward? Got something digging up your vegetable patch? I know there's been a creature running amok. We lost a couple goats last month."

"I don't have any livestock, so that hasn't been an issue." I could tell she expected me to elaborate. I had no intention of offering one word more than was necessary though. I didn't trust witches. Never did.

The interior of the farmhouse seemed like a slice of Americana, except for the elements that were clearly designed for its magical inhabitants. The deep-set fireplace housed a cauldron, the kitchen shelves were heaving with glass jars filled with herbs, and a black cat draped itself along the windowsill, its tail dangling above the sink. The strong scent of alcohol lingered in the air, and I wondered whether Penelope had been overindulging before I arrived. The thought of a drunk witch with a shotgun unsettled me.

"Make yourself at home." Penelope inclined her head toward the rectangular wooden table. Despite the smell, she seemed steady on her feet and stone cold sober.

I pulled out a chair, one of six. "How many witches live here?"

"Six. All family."

"Are you the only witches in Fairhaven?"

She sniffed. "The only ones worth knowing. You live alone, is that it?" she persisted. "Don't want unwelcome suitors turning up at all hours?"

"That's certainly one reason." There'd be no suitors. I made the mistake of trying to date a few years ago; I started and ended with a vampire by the name of Balthazar. Neither one of us seemed sure whether he was amenable to my requests because he genuinely liked me or because I was inadvertently influencing him. In the end, it didn't seem worth the confusion, and I ended things.

"It's hot out there. Care for a cold drink?"

"No, thank you." I didn't trust her not to lace it with some sort of truth potion and wheedle my secrets out of me.

Penelope settled in the chair across from me. "How big is your property?"

"Bigger than this one," I said.

"I've got five acres."

"As much as that?"

"Most of it's behind the house. There's even a pond."

"Not koi, I imagine."

She grimaced. "Good grief, no. What do you take me for? We did have a group of turtles for a bit, but they've been gone for months now."

"They migrated to another body of water?" Fairhaven seemed to have no shortage of water sources.

Penelope seemed disinterested in the fate of the turtles. "Couldn't say."

"I've never known a witch who kept her own chickens."

She studied me. "How many have you known?"

"Enough." I met her inquisitive gaze and was struck by the color of her eyes; they shone like two newly minted pennies.

"What's your budget?" she asked. "Wards don't come cheap, and we could use the money."

It seemed Kane wasn't wrong about the meager lottery winnings. "I was hoping we could come to an arrangement. I'm short on cash."

Penelope grunted. "Of course you are. Well, we've been dealing with troubles of our own. I'm not sure I can spare the hands if it's not going to be worth our while."

"What kind of trouble? You haven't lost any witches recently, have you?"

She rested her elbows on the table's edge. "What makes you ask that?"

"I heard about a local girl that went missing."

Penelope blew a gunmetal curl from her eye, and it bounced straight back into view. "Wouldn't be the first one, but no, we haven't lost any of ours, thank goddess."

"There have been other missing girls?"

"I've heard rumors of vampires trafficking young women

in and out of Fairhaven." Her expression soured. "I steer clear of bloodsuckers as a rule, though, so I can't help you with any details."

The kitchen door opened, and a middle-aged woman entered the house. She was petite, with reddish-brown hair tied in a messy bun and the same bright copper eyes as Penelope.

"This is my daughter, Sierra." She waved a hand at me. "Sierra, this is Lorelei Clay. She needs a ward."

Sierra bowed her head in greeting. "Nice to meet you."

Two more women trailed into the kitchen behind Sierra. They appeared older than Sierra, but sometimes it was hard to tell with witches.

"Margaret, Brenda, meet Lorelei," Penelope said. "Margaret and Brenda are my younger sisters."

I waved. Two to go.

"There's a tree down," Margaret said. "Half of it fell straight into the pond."

"We'll use it for firewood come winter," Penelope said. "Tell Kelsey to get the chainsaw."

"We'll need to wait until she's finished with her other chores," Brenda said.

Penelope turned back to me. "We had a storm blow through the other night. Wreaked havoc."

"Really? I didn't hear it."

"Might've been localized," Penelope said. "Downtown Fairhaven is somewhat sheltered, hence the name."

Another witch wandered into the kitchen from outside. Her face and T-shirt were splattered with dirt and there was a sheen of sweat across her brow. The smell of alcohol intensified with her arrival.

"I've had enough of this," she declared, setting a large bucket on the floor next to the door. "I'm not cut out for all this manual labor." She seemed to notice me for the first time.

"Oh, hello. I didn't realize we had company." She shot a guilty glance at the bucket.

"Lorelei Clay, this is my niece, Kelsey," Penelope said.

Kelsey's hair was flaming red, and her lightly wrinkled face suggested late thirties. "I didn't realize we were expecting company, Aunt Pen. You should've said so." With a casual air, she opened the door and placed the bucket outside. She continued to hold the door open as a sixth woman crossed the threshold carrying a basket covered by a checkered cloth. A blonde ponytail poked out from the back of a baseball cap.

"It's as hot as the devil's balls today." She stopped short when she noticed me, and her cheeks grew flushed. "I mean, it's *very* hot outside."

"My younger sister, Phaedra," Sierra said through thinned lips.

Phaedra looked to be close to my age, maybe slightly younger. "Hello."

"She's been away," Penelope added, "which explains the colorful language she picked up during her absence."

Phaedra ducked her head, clearly embarrassed. "Where would you like the eggs, mother?"

Penelope turned to regard her. "How many today?"

"Fewer than yesterday."

Penelope's hand tightened into a fist. "Leave them on the counter. I'll deal with them later."

"Are you making moonshine?" I asked.

You could've heard a pin drop.

Penelope's lip curled. "Now that's a strange question."

"I recognize the smell. My grandfather had a friend who liked to make his own."

Phaedra burst into laughter. "Oh, go on. Tell her."

"I can hardly hide the smell," Kelsey said. "I reek like a liquor store."

"We can send a jar home with you, if you like," Brenda added.

I waved a hand airily. "No, it's not my thing, thanks, but the smell brought back some childhood memories." Pops didn't drink, but his friend Mitch did. They'd sit outside on the stoop and trade stories while Mitch drank his stash. I'd listen from my bedroom window and wonder how some people found the strength to wake up every day and keep going.

Penelope's lip relaxed. "This batch is a bit strong, so probably for the best."

"Making moonshine on top of everything else," I commented. "You must be busy."

Kelsey dragged her forearm along her brow to wipe away the sweat. "No kidding. It would be great if we could afford to hire someone so I could rejoin humanity. I haven't been on a date in ages."

"We had Georgia, but she's gone now," Brenda volunteered.

I didn't miss the looks exchanged by Margaret and Sierra. "Who's Georgia?" I asked.

Penelope's lips grew taut. "She was in our employ, but no longer."

"Another witch?"

"A brownie," Brenda said. "Real pretty too. Light brown hair and these enormous brown eyes."

At least I knew who the chatty one was in the coven. "I could use help around my house. Is she available for work or did she leave for another job?"

"Thought you were short on cash," Penelope pointed out.

"I am, but my house is huge. I figured I could offer her room and board in exchange for light duties." A feasible lie.

Penelope seemed to accept my answer. "She left two months ago in the company of her new boyfriend, who didn't like that she was working for witches. Didn't leave a forwarding address."

"That's too bad."

"Werewolf," Margaret said with a disapproving sniff. "Why couldn't he at least have been an Arrowhead? Then she could've stayed here."

"Arrowhead is the local pack?" I asked.

Margaret nodded. "They live in the trailer park northwest of here, just south of the highway."

Penelope snapped her fingers, appearing irritated by the chatter. "Brenda, fetch a pen and paper. Miss Clay was about to give me the details of her property for the ward."

"You haven't quoted me a price," I said.

"Can't do that without knowing more about your property," Penelope said, keeping her gaze fixed on me. "What's your address? I'll have one of the girls drop it by with instructions when it's ready."

"Bluebeard's Castle."

Sierra flinched at the mention of the house. "I didn't realize you're the one who bought it."

"You know it?"

"Everybody around here knows it. Been sitting empty for decades," Brenda answered for Sierra.

"That's a lot of house for one person," Margaret said.

"I like my space."

Phaedra smiled. "Try living in a farmhouse with a coven of witches."

"We have acres of land around us," Penelope said with a sweeping gesture. "Just go outside if you're feeling smothered."

Phaedra opened the cupboard and retrieved a glass. "Where do you think I am half the time? I'm just glad it's summer. I can't handle the cold."

I was no stranger to the cold, although I agreed with Phaedra. Not a fan.

They seemed friendly enough as far as witches were concerned; I decided to go ahead and ask the other question burning my tongue. "While I'm here, any chance you could do a locator spell?"

"That'll cost as much as a ward," Penelope said.

I didn't doubt it, but I needed to exhaust all the avenues in relation to Ashley.

"Who are you trying to find?" Kelsey asked. "A man?"

"Gods, no. I'm not in the market for a relationship. I'm pouring all my energy into my house."

"That's a safer bet than a man," Sierra said, nodding agreeably.

"There's a missing young woman by the name of Ashley Pratt. I have one of her belongings with me, if that would help."

"It certainly increases the chances of success," Penelope said. "Sierra is our resident expert on those sorts of spells."

Sierra's face grew flushed. "I'm not that much better than the rest of you."

Penelope patted her hand. "Don't be so modest."

I pulled Ashley's bracelet from my pocket and placed it on the table. "This is special to her."

Sierra's long, elegant fingers stretched to retrieve the gold chain. She dangled it in the air, holding it up to the light for a better view. "Pretty trinket."

"It's one of her favorite pieces."

"I'll do my best." Sierra rose to her feet and padded to the kitchen. "This will only take a few minutes."

Kelsey eyed me curiously from her place against the wall. "Where are you from?"

"Most recently, London."

Kelsey gasped. "I've always wanted to go there. And Paris. Have you been to Paris? I want to try every pastry they bake."

Brenda shot her daughter a silencing look. "You'll have to

excuse Kelsey. We don't get too many visitors at the farm. She's forgotten her manners."

I turned my attention to Sierra in the kitchen, who was currently frowning at the marble mortar on the counter. "Is there a problem?"

"I'm not getting anything at all. I usually get a hint of a location, if nothing else. A smell. A glimpse of surroundings. A sound. But all I'm getting are the sounds around me."

"We're still charging you," Penelope said.

"Two favors it is." I wouldn't dream of trying to cheat Penelope Bridger; she'd probably turn me into a toad and then charge me for it.

I left the farm feeling dispirited over Ashley. At least I'd have my ward.

CHAPTER 8

Dinner was a simple affair. A four-ounce salmon and a side of asparagus. A glass of water to wash it down. I would've preferred a glass of wine, but my current budget didn't allow it. A huge fixer-upper hadn't been the most brilliant decision I'd ever made. I was beginning to wonder whether I'd been under the influence of a magical substance when I made the purchase. I'd been to a bar the night before; it was within the realm of reason that someone had dropped an illicit substance into my glass.

No. I couldn't blame anyone else. This had been my decision, similar to the ones I'd made many times before. A knee-jerk reaction. An emotional response to an unwanted situation. And now there were consequences to my rash decision.

I was in a town teeming with supernaturals, where even some of the humans seemed aware of our existence. If Pops had known there were places like this, he never said.

While I ate, I sat at the table and leafed through *A Complete History of Fairhaven*. "It can't be that complete," I murmured. "The copyright date is 1979." A quick flip to the index showed no references to vampires or werewolves either.

I carried my empty plate to the sink, preparing to dive into the book.

"At last I've found you!" a voice cried.

I dropped the plate into the sink, and it cracked in half. I spun around, my heart pounding mercilessly. "Matilda, what the hell?" I blew out a breath to steady my heart rate. "How did you find me?"

The crone cackled, as crones were wont to do. "You left London. You didn't leave the planet. I'm mystical, annwyl. I can always hunt you down." She smiled at her own joke. Matilda of the Night, or the Night Mallt in Welsh, once rode with the Wild Hunt. She and I met at a gathering in London a couple years ago and hit it off due to our common natures. I hadn't expected to like her, but Matilda surprised me. I'd moved to Fairhaven on a whim and hadn't thought to tell her. I hadn't thought to tell anyone.

"You could've given me a warning. I would've stocked the liquor cabinet," I said.

Matilda's gaze raked over me. "You look tired. Nightmares?"

"It's not been too bad lately."

"That's something, at least. We all need a break from what plagues us." She sat at the kitchen table. "Where's your hospitality? I'm positively parched after my long journey."

"As you said, you're mystical. How long could your journey be?"

She stretched her thin lips over gums. "You should get a cat."

"I don't want a cat."

"I can understand why you refuse a dog, but a cat is good company."

"I don't want a cat." I didn't want any additional responsibility or complications.

"Nonsense. Anyone with half a brain wants a cat."

"I'm allergic."

She shook her head, knowing perfectly well I was full of shit. "This is a wonderful part of the country. You made a good choice. The Wild Acres are exquisite. Have you been?"

"Not yet. Been busy fixing up the house. You didn't try to hunt, did you?" Matilda had a habit of creating a mess in her wake—and by a mess, I meant a trail of bloodhounds and wayward souls.

"No, no. I will leave the restless spirits here in your care." She inclined her head. "I noticed a few outside. Stubborn, are they?"

"They've chosen to stay, and I've chosen to let them."

Matilda cackled again. "You always have been a soft touch. Perhaps your next incarnation will be tougher."

I sighed. "I'm as tough as I need to be." At this rate, I'd be out of teabags by the end of the week. I'd managed to go for months without replenishing my stash when I didn't have visitors.

"What's with the moat in this day and age?"

"It's an original feature."

"It's stupid and unnecessary. Why not fill it in? You can create a lovely floral border with it."

"I might. I haven't decided yet." I still clung to images of me floating around the outside of the house on the back of a blowup swan. Black, of course. "Since you're here, would you mind helping me with a problem?"

"The walls just need a lick of paint, and they'll be perfectly presentable for guests."

"I'm not talking about the house."

Her brow furrowed. "Oh, why not? Because you're in dire need of help with this monstrosity."

"Gee, thanks. Now I know who to call for unconditional support."

Matilda's knobby fingers wrapped around the cup. "Have you found yourself in trouble already? Anything like London?"

"No, nothing like London." I didn't want to talk about my experience there. It had been fine, until it wasn't. Everywhere was fine until it wasn't.

"Would you mind a weary guest for one night?"

"If the weary guest doesn't mind helping me track down a missing girl."

Her eyes brightened, as I knew they would. "We're hunting? Why didn't you say so?"

"She's alive, or at least I think she is."

Matilda didn't bother to hide her disappointment. The hunt was more enjoyable for her when the prey was already dead. I didn't judge her for it. The Night Mallt had once been a young woman whose beauty rivaled Helen of Troy. Hunting was her passion; accordingly, she was alleged to have told the gods she'd rather not leave this earth if there'd be no hunting in the Great Beyond. Once she reached a ripe old age, Matilda was tasked with riding with the hounds of the Wild Hunt, forever chasing lost souls to their final destinations. The legends state that Matilda regretted her choice, but I knew for a fact that wasn't true. Matilda was never in her element more than when she was on the hunt.

"The girl's name is Ashley Pratt," I continued. "Her brother is searching for her and asked for my help."

Matilda eyed me. "And you agreed?"

"I did."

"Is he bedworthy?"

"Nobody says bedworthy, Matilda. Not now, and not in ancient times."

"I say it, and that's all that matters. Now stop avoiding the question."

"I didn't agree because he's good looking."

She slapped a palm flat on the table. "Aha! He is attractive."

"No, I mean." I took a moment to start again. "Steven

Pratt is a twenty-five-year-old human male. I have no romantic interest in him. He's fixing my computer."

Her gaze drifted to the computer on the nearby table. "Are you certain he knows what he's doing? He isn't some technical charlatan?"

"I'm choosing to trust him."

She cocked her head, studying me. "How odd. Do you have a picture of the fair missing maiden?"

I shared the photo on my phone that Steven had sent to me. Matilda examined the image. "Very pretty. Wouldn't surprise me if a god rode off with her to make her his bride."

"That sort of thing doesn't happen anymore."

"Says you."

"I have one of her personal items. It might help the hounds to have her scent."

Matilda wiggled her fingers in a give-it-here gesture. I handed over the bracelet; the crone brought it to her nostrils and inhaled deeply.

"She is not so innocent."

"Does it matter?"

"No, I only meant she wouldn't be part of a virgin sacrifice."

"Oh, fair point." It wasn't as though there were many volcanoes in this region, active or otherwise. "Can you tell me anything else?"

She tossed the bracelet on the table. "I'm not a medium, Lorelei. I don't do parlor tricks."

I tucked the bracelet back in my pocket for safekeeping. I hoped to return it to Ashley in person one day.

"You should know, cariad, there've been rumors."

"There are always rumors."

"These rumors shouldn't be ignored." She hesitated. "A great power is rising."

I rolled my eyes. "Another day, another demon summoning."

Matilda shook her head slowly. "Nothing of that nature. This is bigger than one demon."

Her somber expression gave me pause. "What kind of power?"

"I don't know the details, only that we would be wise to stay hidden."

"Well, that's no hardship for me. It's the whole point of moving here."

"Take care and don't flaunt your powers." She laughed lightly. "I forget who I'm talking to. There's no fear of that."

"Speaking of demon summoning, know anyone by the name of Kane Sullivan?"

"Should I?"

I shrugged. "Just curious."

"What did he smell like?"

"Evergreen." I smiled. "But that's probably because we were in the middle of the woods."

"Meeting strangers in the woods, eh? How very fairy tale of you."

"Technically, the cocktail lounge was in the middle of the woods." And he was no Prince Charming.

"A cocktail lounge? You should have said so."

"We're not going. It's full of unsavory characters. He keeps a healer on his payroll for the fights."

She gave me a pointed look. "You're not making me want to go any less with that description."

I slipped on my shoes that I'd left by the front door. "While we're riding, tell me if you sense a vortex or some other power source," I told her.

"Wouldn't you be able to tell?"

"Not always. It depends on what it is. There seems to be something here that attracts supernaturals, but I haven't found any evidence of it."

"Hmm," Matilda said.

"What?"

"I wonder whether that's what enabled me to find you so easily. I asked, and the universe answered." She opened her arms.

"Is it usually harder than that?"

"Well, this is the first time I've hunted you. For others, it isn't so instantaneous though. Usually involves an offering."

Food for thought.

I walked outside to see her spectral horse, a black mare with fearsome red eyes.

"Gorgeous. What happened to the last one?"

"This one suits my personality better."

"She rides relentlessly?"

"She bites."

I smiled. "Where are the hounds?"

She waved a hand at the forest behind the house. "Crawling your woods." She stuck her fingers in her mouth and blew a shrill whistle. "We'll need them now."

"They don't like me, remember?" Dogs in general didn't like me, which was one of the reasons I avoided suburban neighborhoods. Everybody had a dog there.

"They'll like you if I tell them to. Besides, these aren't regular hounds. They'll recognize you for who you really are."

I didn't want to think about that. "I appreciate your help, Matilda."

"No need to thank me. This is exactly the kind of activity I was hoping to partake in. You've given an old crone a moment of happiness, Lorelei. That's very difficult to do."

"Glad I could be of service."

Matilda gestured for me to mount the horse first. I didn't have much experience with horses—my abilities didn't involve them—and I was mildly embarrassed when Matilda felt the need to give my bottom a shove. Up and over my leg went until I was stable on the horse's back. Matilda positioned herself in front of me.

"Taller than my motorcycle," I remarked.

"Hold on to me, cariad, or you might find yourself rolling down that steep hill of yours. On second thought, perhaps you'll end up on the doorstep of some handsome farmer. Might be worth giving you a shove."

"There are no handsome farmers."

She cackled. "I suppose your plan is to remain celibate forever. A pity, a pretty woman like you. There are all manner of hunts, Lorelei, and some are almost as wild as mine."

I leaned forward as though straining to listen. "What was that? I can't hear you over the wind."

Laughing, she spurred the horse onward. "How I've missed you, cariad."

We rode to the forest, and two hounds joined us en route. They were fearsome beasts—the size of gorillas, with powerful limbs and razor-sharp teeth. Their red eyes glowed with the same intensity as the mare's.

Matilda leaned over to hold out the bracelet for them. Each hound inhaled the scent of the bracelet and charged.

"Are they running because they smell something?" I asked.

"I suppose we're about to find out." She jammed her heels into the mare's side, and off we went.

The hounds were fast and agile. They leapt over fallen trees with grace and avoided collisions with low-hanging branches. Matilda and her horse were equally adept. I felt mildly nauseous, but I refused to say so. I'd never hear the end of it.

The deepest part of the forest was eerily quiet; it seemed as though every living creature sensed the arrival of members of the Wild Hunt and made themselves scarce. Not that I blamed them. If I didn't know Matilda, I'd hide too.

In the six months since my arrival, I hadn't yet managed to hike in Wild Acres or kayak the Delaware River. I'd intended to take time in the spring to enjoy outdoor activities when the weather was more favorable, but the Castle seemed to occupy me day and night.

Or maybe that was an excuse to stay inside and away from people. Sometimes even I was unsure of my true motivation.

I caught the literal tail end of rabbits and squirrels and foxes, all manner of woodland creatures. It was nighttime now, too late for hikers, and the campsites were miles away. It was pitch dark; nobody would see us even if they were here. Nobody alive anyway.

The moon stared down at us with what seemed like a disapproving gaze. Or maybe that was me projecting. I didn't like to ask friends like Matilda for assistance. It wasn't fair to keep my distance but then rely on them when it suited me.

The hounds pressed their noses to the ground and finally stopped in front of a massive oak tree. The tree was remarkable for its position; alone in the middle of a clearing, its long, substantial branches seemed to mark the area as its own territory.

The hounds howled in unison.

"She's here?" I asked, climbing down to the ground.

"She was." Matilda approached the tree with cautious steps. "But not anymore."

"How long ago?"

Matilda gave me a dismissive look. "Do I look like a wolf shifter to you? I have no sense of time when it comes to the living, only the sorrowful dead. But I can tell you the trail ends here."

"Thank you, Matilda."

The crone offered a smile of crooked yellow teeth. "I was helpful then?"

"Very."

"Now we can stop at the unsavory cocktail lounge?"

"Another time." One run-in with Kane Sullivan was quite enough for this week.

"Another establishment then?"

"Do you have money? There's a liquor store that might still be open." We'd have to leave the hounds and horse at the Castle though.

The crone mounted the mare. "What need do I have of money? I'll simply hunt down a good bottle of wine and take it."

"I'll leave that part to you. I live here now. I can't be involved in any crimes."

Matilda cackled again. "Such a waste of power. If only they knew."

I hauled myself onto the back of the horse, thinking about Ashley. She'd been here recently, which meant she likely hadn't gone back to town from Monk's. Somewhere between Monk's and this oak tree, the young woman vanished.

I needed a werewolf, preferably one who knew the area well. Good thing I knew just where to find one.

CHAPTER 9

The Arrowhead wolf pack lived in a horseshoe-shaped trailer park in the wooded outskirts of town. Dirt roads connected the park to the highway to the north and the town to the southeast. There were about three dozen trailers total, which suggested a decent-sized pack for a town as small as Fairhaven.

I parked my truck alongside the dirt road and proceeded on foot. I surveyed the trailers for the biggest one, or any obvious sign of the alpha's residence. My gaze landed on a trailer with a looped iron symbol affixed to the front door—the Greek symbol for alpha. Easy enough. The unit and outside space were identical in size to the others. Fairness and equality were more important to this alpha; good to know.

I strode toward the front door, noting the silence. Given the number of homes, there should've been a smattering of neighborhood noises. It was a warm, sunny day. School was out for summer. Why weren't the children running around outside?

A voice stopped me in my tracks. "He's not home."

I turned to see a buff thirty-something male with dark brown hair and an exaggerated brow standing on the dirt road. "Any idea when he'll be back?" I asked, walking closer to him.

He eyed me with suspicion. "Nope."

"It's so quiet here. Where is everybody?"

"Oh, you'd like to meet everybody?" His mouth split into a crooked smile. "That can be arranged." His whistle ripped through the eerie silence.

Werewolves emerged from every nook and cranny of the trailer park. It reminded me of the scene from *The Wizard of Oz* when the munchkins came out of hiding to greet Dorothy and Glinda. The thought of the werewolves in green overalls and argyle knee socks amused me more than it should have, especially right now when a dozen werewolves were circling me.

"What's so funny?" the whistling werewolf demanded.

"You're surrounded by the Arrowhead pack," another werewolf chimed in. "You should be begging for mercy, not laughing." He was taller and broader than his friend. His arms looked like they'd chopped an entire national forest in their lifetime.

Someone in the dirty dozen shushed him. "You shouldn't have said that."

"The part about the pack or the vague threat of harm?" I asked. "I know you're werewolves, so he wasn't giving away any secrets."

"Told you she wasn't no human," a voice hissed behind me.

"I don't like this," an older werewolf growled. "Something's off about her."

"Is this how you greet all visitors to the neighborhood?" Not that I was one to talk; I had a gate and a moat.

A werewolf with spiked brown hair sniffed the air. She sported a black tank top with the AC/DC logo and denim shorts that revealed a pair of muscular legs that had probably crushed more male torsos than I'd ever seen. To be fair, I hadn't seen many up close and personal. I found relationships—as well as the male torsos that accompanied them—were best avoided.

"You don't smell familiar," the female werewolf said.

"Because we're strangers," I told her.

"All the more reason why you shouldn't be here," the beefy werewolf said.

The spiky-haired werewolf scrunched her nose. "Bert's right. She smells wrong. Anybody else catch a whiff?"

"Hey, the water heater in my house is iffy," I replied, mildly insulted, although I knew what she really meant.

"This is our land," the whistling werewolf said, spitting on the ground between us.

I gave the defiled ground a pointed look. "In that case, you should treat it better."

His eyes glazed over with a golden tint. Note to self: do not insult werewolves on their home turf *about* their home turf.

"I think we ought to roll up the welcome mat, Paulie," Bert said. "What do you think?"

Twelve werewolves were too numerous to fight at once, even for me. Unless I wanted to reveal myself, though, there was no choice. I would've happily opted for flight over fight, but they were currently blocking all the escape routes. I decided to try one more tack.

I held up my hands in acquiescence. "I'm not here to fight."

"Then you shouldn't have come," Paulie said.

He was right. I made a mistake in coming here without warning. I should've done my research first, gotten more information about the pack. Arranged an introduction. Lesson learned. As long as they didn't shift, I could still salvage this.

"I was hoping…" I didn't get to finish my request. I saw a blur of movement to my left and ducked before a large sneaker made contact with the side of my head. As the leg swung over me, I popped back up and grabbed the ankle, twisting it into an unnatural position. The werewolf's howl coincided with a snapping sound.

I was hopeful the bold move would dissuade the others. I should've known better. Werewolves didn't back down from a fight, certainly not one they were confident they could win.

Two of them shifted.

Well, damn.

The large grey wolves immediately dropped to their bellies and began to whine.

"What's the matter with you two?" Bert snapped.

Paulie stared at them for a beat before turning his incredulous eyes to me. "What'd you do to them?"

"Nothing." Werewolves' senses were heightened in their animal forms, which was why the two on the ground found themselves cowering. Although they still wouldn't be able to identify me, their primal instincts told them to be very, very afraid.

"She's a witch," another werewolf cried with a fiery look in her brown eyes. The middle-aged brunette was average height with a broader than average build. Powerful biceps were visible beneath her green Pocono Mountains T-shirt.

"Now that's just insulting," I replied.

"She's not a witch," someone said firmly. Anna, the werewolf from Monk's, pushed her way through the pack to stand beside Paulie.

I held my breath, waiting to see whether she'd share the details of our last encounter.

"Witches around here smell like manure and lavender," Anna continued. "I don't know what she is, but it isn't a witch."

The wolves on the ground started to howl like they were being dragged to the vet, which made the others uneasy.

Anna tugged Paulie's arm. "We can't have them howling like that."

His gaze slid to me. "You need to go. Now."

"On one condition. I need to borrow your best trackers. I'm searching for a missing woman by the name of Ashley Pratt."

He scoffed. "Who do you think you are, coming here and demanding trackers?"

I pressed on. "Ashley is local. The police don't think she wants to be found."

"Maybe they're right," Anna said.

"Her brother is confident that she didn't take off, and I believe him."

Paulie seemed to relax a bit once he realized I wasn't here to smite them. "We've heard rumors recently. Somebody's trafficking runaways."

"Any idea who this somebody is?"

"Vampires," he said.

Despite Otto's protest, the same rumor was making the rounds through the various supernatural groups. Maybe there was something to it after all.

"West told us not to talk about it since it's all speculation," Paulie continued. "He doesn't want to start a war with them."

Understandable. "Thanks, Paulie. I appreciate your cooperation." Just because I scared the daylights out of them didn't mean I couldn't show gratitude. "How many trackers can you spare?"

He shook his lowered head. "Can't. It's got to be West's call."

"Then tell West I need to see him as soon as he gets back. He can find me at Bluebeard's Castle."

The mention of the bluestone manor got his attention. His head jerked up. "That's you?"

"That's me."

Paulie laughed. "You moved into the Ruins?"

I crossed my arms. "People call it the Castle."

"Idiots call it the Castle," Bert said. "We call it the Ruins."

"It's habitable," I argued.

"And Monique is actually pretty if you squint enough," Paulie shot back.

The spikey-haired werewolf snarled at him.

Another werewolf stepped forward. I'd noticed him during the fight because he'd backed away from the circle, unwilling to engage. "You need help over there? We've got guys looking for steady work."

"I'm good right now, but I'll let you know." I had no use for werewolves on my property. In constant close proximity, his 'guys' would spend their time with their tails between their legs, avoiding my presence. They couldn't help themselves; I made their hairs stand on end. Or smelled 'wrong.'

Relief spread across Paulie's face when I started toward my truck. I didn't enjoy injecting fear into anybody; it was one of the reasons I kept to myself, but it came in handy on occasions like this one. Thanks to Pops, I'd learned to defend myself in childhood without the need to resort to my powers. One of the perks of being raised by humans. It was, by far, one of the most valuable lessons he ever taught me.

I parked the truck outside the gate to the Castle—*not* the Ruins, weary from my tense interactions with the pack. That meeting could've gone very wrong. It had been a misstep on my part; I was out of practice dealing with the living.

A text from Steven popped up, asking whether tomorrow morning was a convenient time to work on my computer. I replied with a thumbs-up emoji. Why use words when a cartoon symbol will suffice?

As I reached the front porch, the sound of a car drew my attention. For a moment, I worried the werewolves had followed me home. I watched with trepidation as a black sedan with tinted windows parked behind my truck. The car door opened, frightening off the large blackbird perched on the gate. A petite woman with bright blue hair emerged from the vehicle. She approached the house, flanked by two men in black kaftans. I couldn't help but smile when they reached the bridge and were forced to walk in a single file line for the next few feet.

"Can I help you?" I asked, once they were safely within earshot.

"No, but I might be able to help you," the woman said. Her blue hair contrasted nicely with her flawless porcelain skin. "Camryn Sable at your service. Kane Sullivan sent me."

I was almost afraid to ask my next question. "What kind of service?"

"You're searching for someone, and I'm very good at finding people."

"Don't be uncivilized," Nana Pratt said behind me. "Invite her in. She might be able to find my Ashley."

I exhaled. "You're welcome to come in."

"Not yet," Camryn said. "The shamans need to go in first."

I cut a glance at the man to her right. "You brought your own shamans?"

"I always bring them for smudging when it's a new building to me." She pressed the pads of her fingers to her cheeks. "Negative energy irritates my skin."

The shamans brushed past me, dried sage in hand.

Ray observed them from the corner of the porch. "Can they hurt us?"

I shook my head silently so as not to draw Camryn's attention. She clearly wasn't willing to take any chances, and I had a feeling she'd draw the line at ghosts, even ones as harmless as Ray and Nana Pratt.

"Downstairs only," I called over my shoulder. Camryn

wouldn't be venturing upstairs, and I didn't like the idea of strange shamans crawling around my bedroom.

"Are your smoke detectors sensitive?" Camryn asked. "If so, you might want to switch them off until they're done."

"It'll be fine." I didn't even have working smoke detectors yet.

After a few minutes, the shamans emerged from the house and gave Camryn the green light. Only then did she cross the threshold, dismissing the shamans.

Standing in the foyer, she inhaled deeply. "I love the scent of sage, don't you?"

"Not particularly. Can I offer you anything to eat or drink?" Given the shaman show, my instincts told me the answer would be a hard pass.

"That won't be necessary. I always carry snacks with me." Camryn opened her bag and produced a small box in bright colors.

"Are those Nerds?"

"Yep." She tipped back her head and tapped the bottom of the box. "I started eating them as a reward to stop smoking, and now I can't stop."

I had fond memories of conning my grandfather into buying me Nerds as rewards for good grades. I didn't have much growing up, but at least I had the occasional treat.

"Let's get down to business," Camryn continued. "You're looking for a young lady. I have certain skills that might help you find her."

I had to admit, that sounded promising, especially in light of recent dead ends. "I don't have a lot of furniture yet. Why don't we sit in the kitchen?"

I noticed that Camryn ogled the interior less than others who'd been admitted. She sat at the table and removed a pack of tarot cards from her Chanel purse.

My mind immediately conjured up a memory of Gunther Saxon in the cemetery. "You're an assassin?"

Her eyebrows squished together without forming any creases on her forehead. The magic of Botox, or maybe just plain magic. "Who did you meet?"

"I'm not at liberty to say." I wasn't sure why I felt compelled to protect Gunther. He didn't seem particularly shy about his personal details.

"It was Gunther, wasn't it?" She clucked her tongue. "It's always Gun. I don't know how he's managed to live this long; I swear."

"You know Gunther?"

She shuffled the cards. "Yes, of course. We're cousins."

I motioned to the deck. "And you're a mage who works with tarot cards, like Gunther."

She shot me a prim look. "I'm a member of La Fortuna, a society of mages that channels our magic through the cards."

"You say mages."

She cut me a quick glance. "You say magi?"

I shrugged. "I'm open to either one." I'd never heard of their society. "You don't use yours as weapons?"

"I didn't say that." She fanned the cards in an arc across the table. "I also channel the cards the more traditional way."

"For information."

Keeping her gaze on the cards, she nodded. "Mr. Sullivan thought my skills might be of use to you."

"Does everybody in this town work for him?"

"Nobody except the staff at the lounge. I owed him a favor, which he called in for you." Her eyes flicked to me briefly, almost accusatory, before returning to the cards.

"I'm not sure how reading my cards will help us find Ashley. I don't even know her."

"I'm not going to read your cards." She straightened in the chair. "I understand she has a blood relative here."

"Steven isn't..." I stopped abruptly. "You mean Nana Pratt."

Camryn tossed another Nerd into her mouth. "Steven told

a friend that his grandmother's ghost persuaded you to help him." She shrugged. "Word gets around."

Fairhaven was worse than a college sorority.

On cue, the older woman materialized. "Did you summon me?"

I gave her a sidelong look. "You were listening, weren't you?"

"From outside the house, I swear. I wasn't breaking the rules."

Camryn watched me with a curious gleam in her eye. "You're speaking to them now."

"Ashley's grandmother is here, Nana Pratt."

Camryn dumped another batch of Nerds into her mouth. "I always wanted the ability to commune with spirits."

"It can be intrusive."

Camryn fanned the cards across the table. Her fingernails were embellished with fake diamonds, at least I assumed they were fake. "Choose a card, Mrs. Pratt," she said.

The older ghost studied the backsides of the cards as though she could see through them. For all I knew she could. Finally, she tapped one in the middle.

My finger cut through her wispy one. "She said this one."

"Two more, please."

Nana Pratt selected two more, which I communicated, and Camryn dutifully turned them over.

I took the opportunity to clean the dirty dishes in the sink while Camryn scrutinized the three cards. I scrubbed away, wondering what had prompted Kane Sullivan to send the mage. A demon like him had to have an ulterior motive.

"She's alive," Camryn said. Her tone suggested she was vaguely surprised by the revelation.

Nana Pratt's breathing hitched, not that she actually breathed, but she could replicate the sound. "Are you sure?"

Camryn couldn't hear her and continued studying the cards. "Huh, that's interesting."

"What is?" I set the last dish on the drying rack and turned to face her.

"The cards tell me she hasn't left Fairhaven."

"Can they narrow down the location?"

"No, it isn't a locator spell. It works differently, although I thought the reading would provide more clarity." Camryn pondered the cards. "It's like she's both here and not here."

"That's a relief," Nana Pratt said. "It means we should be able to find her, right?" She floated back and forth behind Camryn's chair. "What if Ray and I visited every house in town? We could…" Her gaze met mine, and she stopped talking. "We can't leave, can we?"

I shook my head. "Unfortunately not."

"That's disappointing. I'd very much like to help find my granddaughter."

I offered a sympathetic smile. "You're a good grandma."

"Lucky Ashley. My grandmother used to call me fat and told me no man would ever want me if I didn't grow out of my chubby phase." Camryn gathered her cards into a pile and stuffed them into their packet. "I was ten."

I winced.

"What else can you do with your cards?" I asked. Gunther's display had intrigued me.

Camryn shook her box of Nerds, and I could tell from the lack of sound that it was now empty. She set the box on the table. "A lot."

That was a vague and unhelpful answer, although one I was intimately familiar with. I decided to press a little harder. "Can you make someone froth at the mouth?"

Her mouth formed a thin line. "Did Gun do that again? I keep telling him it's a bad idea."

"Is he the only one who does that?"

"He's the only mage that theatrical. Anybody else would simply give the target a stomach virus and call it a day."

"You don't need cards for that. That's what undercooked chicken is for."

She smirked. "Cards work faster." She clutched her Chanel purse under her arm. "It was a pleasure doing business with you, Miss Clay. My regards to your spirits."

"Thank you," Nana Pratt called, waving after her.

I walked Camryn to the door, curious to see whether the shamans would lay their kaftans across the grass for her to cross. The men, however, were nowhere to be seen.

Camryn craned her neck to look at me as she stepped onto the porch. "Tell me, what do you have that Kane wants?"

"Excuse me?"

"Kane Sullivan doesn't do favors for just anybody."

"He thinks a missing young woman is bad for his business."

Camryn cocked her head, studying me. "He would say that, wouldn't he? Hmm." She turned and sauntered down the steps to the walkway, stepping daintily over any cracks in the pavement.

Ray appeared on the porch. "Why didn't the smoke clear us out?"

"For one thing, you were already outside. There were no spirits inside the house to cleanse."

"What if we'd wandered in unawares?" Nana Pratt asked, moving to join Ray outside.

"Burning sage alone wouldn't have been enough. They'd need more ingredients." It was like Jessie Talbot's wreath; there were a few accurate details but not enough to get the job done.

The elderly woman appeared visibly relieved. "Good to know."

"The smoke can work as a bridge between worlds."

"Which means what?" Ray asked.

"A bridge works in two directions. You can use smoke to

get rid of the spirits you don't want or use it to have positive spirits cross over *to* you."

Nana Pratt pursed her lips, appearing to process the information. "And we're considered positive spirits, so we'd be able to stay?"

"The simple answer is yes."

"I thought shamans were supposed to be women," Ray said. "I saw that in a documentary once."

"Traditionally, they were."

"Well, either way, this is good news," Nana Pratt said.

"It is." Ashley was still alive and, even better, she was in Fairhaven, sort of—that part was ambiguous.

"Are you going to tell Steven?"

"Not yet. I don't want to get his hopes up, and I don't have anything specific to tell him."

"You should call that Mr. Sullivan and thank him," Nana Pratt said. "Is he single?"

"Demons like Kane Sullivan are always single."

"I could understand having trouble finding someone in a huge city like London, but Fairhaven is a small town. It should be easy," Ray mused.

I agreed. It suggested someone was blocking any locator magic. Unfortunately, in a town with this many supernaturals, the list of those with that capability or access to that capability was too long to contemplate.

CHAPTER 10

Steven showed up on schedule the next morning. He carried his version of a toolkit, which was a well-worn brown leather bag that contained whatever items were necessary to revive my aging computer.

He sat at the desk and flexed his fingers, as though preparing to play a piano. My mind flicked to Otto. I still had to uphold my promise to visit the vampire within the next week. It seemed that favors made the world go round in Fairhaven.

"Let me know if you need anything," I said. "I'll be in the living room with headphones and a hammer."

"Sounds like a dangerous combination," Steven remarked.

"You should offer him a drink at the very least," Nana Pratt urged, as I wandered out of the kitchen area. "Maybe scramble a few eggs."

"I'm not playing hostess. That wasn't part of the deal."

The old woman followed behind me, persistent. "It's not about your deal. It's about common decency."

I put on my headphones and started the playlist on my phone. Otto was right about me; I missed playing music. Unfortunately I'd learned that wasn't a safe option for me. I lost myself in music and losing myself wasn't something I could afford to do, so I gave it up.

As I raised the hammer, Nana Pratt positioned herself between me and my chosen nail. I let the hammer drop anyway, and it cut right through her. She gasped, seeming to forget that the tool couldn't actually hurt her. Although her mouth moved, I continued to focus on the plank of wood. She seemed intent on distracting me. I whipped off the headphones and glared at her.

"What is it now?"

"He needs your password," she said.

I turned around to see Steven in the arched doorway behind me. "I need your password," he said.

"I have a password?"

"According to your computer."

Well, crap. "Let me think."

He gave me a lopsided grin. "When's the last time you used it?"

"When I lived in the States. I left it in a storage unit when I moved to England."

Steven grinned. "Yeah, see. Computers don't really last very long. They're like new cars. They depreciate the moment you take them home."

"I think he likes you," Nana Pratt said. "You should date him."

I shot the ghost a silencing look.

"This is a big house. You could fit a dozen children in here."

I ignored her for the sake of my blood pressure. "Can I get you a cup of tea? I'm sorry, but I don't have coffee in the house."

His eyes widened. "How do you function in the morning?"

"Tea has caffeine."

"Not enough. What have you got against coffee?"

"Nothing. I'll drink it on occasion, but it isn't my go-to."

He stared at me for a long beat. "Huh," he finally said. "Is that some sort of diet thing?"

I narrowed my eyes. "Do I seem like someone who should be on a diet?"

"Oh, dear," Nana said, wringing her hands. "He didn't mean to insult you."

"No, not at all," Steven said. "You look like you work out."

"I don't have to work out. Manual labor takes care of it for me." I twirled the hammer in the air.

"I'll have that tea, unless you've changed your mind. Granny Higgins used to make me tea when I was sick."

"Oh, sure. Extoll the virtues of that dreadful woman right in front of me," Nana Pratt moaned.

"It isn't a competition," I whispered to her.

"Of course it is!"

I walked past Steven into the kitchen and filled the kettle. "What's the prognosis?"

Steven reclaimed his seat at the table. "Honestly, I'm not sure this is fixable, but I'll give it my best shot."

I turned on the gas and swiveled to face him. "Let me try a few passwords."

His hands were poised to type, but there was no way I was sharing that information, even if it failed to work. I bumped him off the chair and made a few guesses. The last one worked.

"Have you always been this suspicious of people?" he asked, returning to the seat.

"I don't think it's unreasonable to keep my password private. It's a basic security measure."

"And a single woman can never be too careful," Nana Pratt added, not that her grandson could hear her.

Steven typed on the keyboard and the screen went berserk. "Did you spill something on the keyboard?"

"If I did, it happened years ago."

He opened his leather bag and retrieved a little bottle with a pump mechanism. He proceeded to use it to blow air around the keys. "Do you miss London?" he asked.

"Not really." Although I missed the historical buildings and the sense of a past that many places in America lacked. Steven didn't need to know about my love of history though. He didn't need to know anything about me at all.

"I'd like to travel more," he said. He finished with the air gizmo and was now using a black cloth to wipe down the keyboard and screen. "I promised Ashley I'd take her to Greece someday. She wants to see one of those black sand beaches."

"Those are very cool," I agreed.

He twisted to look at me. "Have you been to one?"

"I have." It had been a good trip with minimal ghostly interaction.

"Cool. When we find Ash, I'm going to tell her that's our next trip. It'll take me time to save the money, but it'll be worth it to see the look on her face." He was smiling at the computer screen now, presumably thinking about how he could make his missing sister happy.

"I told you he's sweet," Nana Pratt said, sighing with contentment. There was so much love packed into that single sigh that I felt my chest constrict in response. The grief of losing Pops ripped through me unexpectedly.

I forced myself to think about Ashley and forget my own pain. Steven sounded so confident that Ashley would return home safely. Even if we found her alive, that didn't mean she'd be unharmed. There were too many unknown variables at this point.

"I've been making the rounds in town," I said. "Talking to people about Ashley."

He nodded, maintaining his focus on the computer.

"He trusts you," Nana Pratt said.

"I wish he wouldn't," I mumbled. I wasn't a detective; this was an informal favor that, in hindsight, I should've refused.

I steeped the teabag, then added milk and one teaspoon of sugar at his request.

"Why do you drink hot tea in the middle of the day when it's eighty degrees outside?" he asked.

"You just asked for a cup," I said accusingly.

He shrugged. "I was feeling nostalgic."

"Iced tea wouldn't make me feel any cooler." Plus, it had become a habit. Iced tea wasn't as prevalent in England; the weather didn't warrant it.

"You'll have to do something about your AC soon," he said. "You'll pass out in here if it gets much hotter. At the very least, buy a few fans, unless, of course, you prefer to suffer."

Ha! It was like he knew me already.

Fans weren't a bad idea though. "I noticed some in Hewitt's the last time I was there." I might as well sell Clark a kidney because I didn't have enough money to afford all the things I needed from his store.

"Yeah, or you could drive further afield to one of the chain stores."

"I'd rather shop local."

"Good girl," Nana Pratt said, nodding her approval.

"You don't need to be here," I told her.

Steven turned his head toward me. "I do if you expect me to fix this thing."

"Sorry, I didn't mean you."

His eyebrows inched up. "Oh. Are you talking to a ghost?"

"Nana Pratt is very invested in your progress."

He broke into a broad grin. "Tell her I'm going to bake lemon tarts using her recipe."

"What's the occasion?" Nana Pratt asked.

"Val Tuckerton is coming over for dinner tomorrow night, and I'd like to impress her," he continued.

Nana Pratt scowled. "I don't like that girl. Tell him she's still involved with Chuck Mahoney. I saw them through the gate. They were parked up the hill smooching in his truck, not that I was spying."

I inhaled, not really wanting to put myself in the middle of this conversation. "Your grandmother says Val is still involved with Chuck Mahoney, and she thinks you deserve better."

Nana nodded firmly. "Darn right I do."

Steven tapped away on the keyboard, seemingly unconcerned. "Tell Nana she's mistaken. Val said she and Chuck are just friends."

Nana Pratt folded her arms in a huff. "Last I checked, friends don't stick their tongues down each other's throats."

"Nana says she's lying."

Steven's expression crumpled. "Well, that's too bad. I thought we were going to make it work this time." He turned back to the computer, shielding his face from me.

I gave Nana Pratt a look of condemnation. She shrugged. "What? He has to know the truth about that hussy."

At least her name wasn't Anya. It would be too disturbing to think about Steven sharing the same taste as Otto Visconti. Then again, Steven wasn't a vampire; his square teeth wouldn't appeal to her.

I returned to the living room to continue my own project. This time Nana Pratt left me in peace. After an hour, Steven declared victory.

"I've held up my end of the bargain. It's working for now, but it's slow. I don't know how long it'll last either. The Internet connection here is garbage, by the way. If I were you, I'd think about getting a new computer before this one kicks the bucket."

"Thank you."

"Fingers crossed for good news about Ashley soon." His eyes glimmered with hope.

"I'm doing what I can."

He hefted the strap of his bag over his shoulder and exited the house.

"He'd better not bake my lemon tart for that tart," Nana Pratt fumed.

"You have to let him make his own mistakes."

"Like Ashley?" she countered.

I fell silent. I didn't have children, but I'd been one, and a difficult one at that. Foster homes didn't pass around easy kids; those they kept.

"There's a redhead snooping around the moat," Ray informed me. "She checked out Steven on his way out too."

"Ooh, is she pretty?" Nana Pratt asked.

I went to the front door to greet Kelsey Bridger. "I guess my ward is ready."

The witch smiled brightly. "It is, but I'll need some of your blood to finalize it."

"That seems unhygienic," Nana Pratt said.

"Do we need to use a special dagger?" I asked.

Kelsey snorted. "No, it isn't a ritual. A pin prick will do." She thrust a glass jar toward me. "Just add it here, and it's done."

The contents of the jar reeked. I didn't dare ask what was in it.

Nana Pratt scrunched her nose. "That looks nasty. You don't have to drink that, do you?"

"It's a ward," Ray said. "It sounds like she'll need to pour it along the property line."

"She'll need more in that case," Nana Pratt said. "What's in the jar won't be enough."

I was itching to tell them to be quiet, but I didn't want to speak to them in front of Kelsey. I had an inherent distrust of witches, and the Bridgers were no exception.

"I can do the honors if you like," Kelsey offered.

"I'll take care of it, thanks."

"Let us know if you need anything else. We're always happy to serve new customers." She spun around and hopped down the steps. "I'm jealous of your moat, by the way. Now our pond seems inadequate."

"It's going to require a lot of maintenance," I said. "I'm wondering if I should fill it in with dirt."

She looked back at me. "Oh, don't do that. In a town like this, it'll be worth having." She crossed the small bridge and sailed through the gate with a childlike spring to her step.

I retreated into the house to add the final ingredient to the mixture.

Nana Pratt held a hand over her eyes. "I can't watch."

"Then don't. You shouldn't even be in the house. You didn't ask permission." I used the tip of a clean knife to pierce my skin. Blood bubbled to the surface, and I dripped it into the jar.

"Nothing happened," Ray said.

"Nothing's supposed to happen. I need to dump it by the gate. The ward will follow the property line automatically."

"That's a neat trick." Ray sounded remarkably underwhelmed for a man with no knowledge of magic until now.

"How do you know it works?" Nana Pratt asked. "Maybe it's like the Emperor's New Clothes."

I bit back a smile. "Were you this suspicious of people when you were alive?"

"You can't trust a redhead," Nana Pratt said. "It's a known fact. No soul."

"I can tell you for a fact that they do have souls."

I carried the jar outside and poured the mixture along the entrance in front of the gate.

"Can we test it?" Ray asked.

"No."

"Call Steven. He's probably only halfway home. Offer to fix him a meal."

I put my hands on my hips to emphasize my statement. "Stop trying to make Steven and I happen."

Nana Pratt harrumphed. "He's a fine young man."

"I agree, but he's not the fine young man for me."

The elderly ghost folded her arms in a huff. "You don't think he's good enough for you."

"It isn't that." At all. Quite the opposite, in fact. "Steven deserves to settle down with a lovely woman who's as normal as they come, not one who speaks to the dead."

"I think it would be nice to have a granddaughter-in-law who could pass along messages to him," Nana Pratt said. "Very convenient."

"So, this is about you, not about Steven," Ray said, mildly amused.

Nana Pratt tightened the belt around her robe. "You know what? You're right. He's a wonderful young man, and I'm not just saying that because he's my grandson, but you need somebody who can meet you where you are. I see that now."

I disagreed. I didn't need somebody to meet me anywhere. I didn't need anybody at all.

I left them to argue and stood on the bridge to observe the state of the moat. Algae had spread across the surface and a faint unpleasant odor permeated my nostrils. The heat and humidity were likely accelerating the growth of harmful bacteria. If I played my cards right, the moat could be another deterrent, except I didn't want a gross ring of mold and mildew around my house. I pictured myself floating on a black inflatable swan across crystal clear water, reading a book in the sunlight.

"Much better," I said quietly.

"Much better? Are we looking at the same moat?" Ray asked.

I hadn't realized he'd joined me on the bridge. "It will be when I finish it."

"You need help."

"I'm fine. There's no rush."

He pointed to the algae. "That gunk tells a different story."

"Patience is a virtue," I said, striding toward the house.

"Except when you're searching for my missing granddaughter," Nana Pratt called after me.

"One more word and I'll make sure you're inside the house the next time Camryn Sable's shamans come to visit," I shouted, walking backward to face them.

Nana Pratt recoiled in horror. "You said sage wouldn't hurt us."

Ray looked down. "She said it can form a bridge between worlds. Like this one."

Nana Pratt cast a sidelong glance at him. "How is it like this one?"

"This bridge connects Lorelei to the outside world."

"This is different," Nana Pratt said. "Lorelei doesn't need a bridge."

Ray's gaze shifted to me. "I think she would agree with you. I think she would be perfectly content with a moat and no bridge."

"That doesn't make any sense," Nana Pratt said. "Then how would she get anywhere?"

I locked eyes with the older ghost. "You're finally starting to understand me, Ray." I turned on my heel and retreated inside the house.

CHAPTER 11

I poked a bubble of paint on the wall, and it flattened. I'd either have to repaint this section or hang a picture over it. Given my current workload, I was voting for a picture.

Slowly I lowered my arm; the fine hairs stood at attention. There was no chill in the air. Far from it—the hot, humid air was smothering me.

Somebody breached the ward.

"You have company, Lorelei!" Nana Pratt's voice rang out. "Oh, and he's very attractive."

I noticed that she'd poked her head through the front door and left the rest of her body on the porch, as though that somehow didn't violate the rule.

"Should I fetch my parasol?" My voice cracked with sarcasm. "Perhaps I can invite him to take a turn around the cemetery."

She glowered at me. "I was only warning you in case your ward didn't work."

"It worked."

"Are you sure? I didn't hear anything."

"There's no wailing siren."

"Too bad. I'd like to be alerted to visitors."

"You seem to be doing a good job of that without any magical assistance," I noted dryly.

Nana Pratt harrumphed and withdrew.

I peeked out the window for a quick look at the visitor. Light brown hair that curled at the edges. A rugged jawline covered in stubble. A blue T-shirt that spanned his six-pack. Tight jeans. Work boots. I knew exactly who he was.

Plastering on my friendliest smile, I opened the door. "You must be West."

The alpha of the Arrowhead pack looked me square in the eye, but I could tell it took great effort. Every fiber of his being was likely telling him to be submissive. I didn't have the heart to tell him resistance was futile.

"Weston Davies, Arrowhead pack."

"Lorelei Clay. Nice to meet you."

He hooked his thumbs through the belt loops of his jeans. "I don't suppose you'd tell me what you are if I asked."

"Is that how we're kicking off this conversation? That's disappointing."

"You're right. Where are my manners?" He glanced skyward. "Beautiful day, isn't it? Temperature's supposed to hit ninety."

"Seems early in the summer for that kind of high."

He shrugged. "Climate change will do that. Did you settle here because this was the only place you could find with a moat?"

"The moat was a bonus. I moved here for the hardware store. Hewitt's has everything." I caught the hint of a smile, but it faded as quickly as it appeared.

"Why do you smell like death?"

"You sure know how to compliment a lady. Is that why you don't have a mate?"

He narrowed his eyes. "What makes you think I don't?"

"Because she would've made herself known when I

showed up on your doorstep." Werewolves were territorial in every respect.

"We're talking about you right now. Don't try to turn the tables." He leaned back to assess me. "You're clearly not a zombie."

"Because zombies don't exist."

His face hardened. "Then what are you?"

"A ghost whisperer."

He huffed. "And I'm surprisingly strong with an affinity for the moon."

I was strong, too, although probably not as strong as the werewolf alpha, not that I had any intention of testing my theory. The less he knew, the better for both of us.

When he realized I wasn't going to say more, he changed tacks. "So, you came by to see me."

"I did."

"Sorry I missed you. I was out of town at a regional meeting with other alphas."

"Sounds like a good time."

His mouth quirked. "The beer was shit, but I managed. Heard you had a good time at Monk's the other night. Met our sweet Anna."

I kept my expression neutral, curious to see what, if anything, Anna had told him. "Yes, she was delightful."

He grunted. "That's not an adjective I'd use, but okay. Sounds like she was drinking and running her mouth more than usual that night."

Good. Anna hadn't spilled the beans, even after my visit to the trailer park. I didn't think she would. Anna had enough nightmares stockpiled in that head of hers to keep me busy for a year. She'd be a fool to say anything.

"She was fine. Chief Garcia came by to make sure neither of us needed a lift to the hospital."

He laughed out loud this time. "Anna's a pain in the ass,

but she's relatively harmless. All bark and no bite, as they say."

"Are you sure about that? Somebody was awfully quick to call the cops once we went outside."

West shrugged. "Okay, so Anna has a temper."

"Seems to run in the pack."

West turned to regard the bright sun. "Are we going to discuss business outside? I'm working up a sweat just standing here."

"It's cooler than inside. No air-conditioning." Werewolves ran hot; unfortunately, I didn't have much to offer to help with that. "Would you like a glass of water?"

"Got anything sweet?"

"Sweet isn't my thing."

His mouth twitched. "Noted."

An idea occurred to me. "Follow me. I know a place that might feel cooler." I figured it couldn't hurt to be accommodating. Despite sweet not being my thing, I'd rather entice werewolves to help with honey.

"Is he really a werewolf?" Nana Pratt asked in a hushed tone, as though West might hear her.

I nodded silently.

"How do you like that?" Ray asked. "Why couldn't I have known that when I was alive?"

Ray had been better off living in ignorance. He would've been frightened, dwelling in the shadow of supernaturals. He would've spent his life in survival mode, never knowing whether to fight or flee.

Much like Steven Pratt, West took his time walking through the house, nearly bumping into a wall as he gaped at the interior.

"This is quite a project. You know this is going to take years to finish, right?"

"I've already been working on it for six months, so yeah; I figure it'll take time." And money. Lots of it.

His laughter shook the dust from the wooden beams that crisscrossed above our heads. "I like a woman who isn't afraid of manual labor. You'd make a decent werewolf."

I filled a glass with water, then escorted him up a flight of stairs to the balcony. There was a stone overhang that kept the area cooler, and the light breeze helped. There were no chairs, but the ledge was sturdy enough to lean against.

"You've kept to yourself. I heard somebody bought the place but not much else until now." He gulped the water so quickly that I regretted not bringing a pitcher.

"I didn't move here to make friends," I said.

"Yet you somehow ended up with a missing one. That's why you need trackers, right? To find a missing local girl?"

"Ashley isn't a friend. I don't even know her."

West raised an eyebrow at that but said nothing.

"A friend of mine picked up her scent in the woods but lost it," I continued. "I'd like to see if your wolves can pick up where she left off."

"The pack hasn't been spending much time in the woods lately. Too much uncertainty with these animal attacks."

"I'm surprised that would keep you out of the woods." A werewolf was fierce enough to take on any animal in the Wild Acres.

"We've picked up strange scents. Whatever's attacking the livestock, I'm not sure it's of this world."

"Yet you haven't felt compelled to investigate?" I would've expected the Arrowhead pack to want to defend their turf from such a threat.

"We've tried," West admitted. "There've been no tracks that we can see. The smell is inconsistent. One day it'll be a dirt and water combo. Another day it'll be musky. That's the reason my pack reacted to you the way they did."

"Rudely?"

He scratched the back of his neck. "I can see how you might think that. There are rules in place at the moment."

"They're only allowed outside to harass visitors?"

He grunted. "I instituted the rules while I was away. I didn't want all hell to break loose while Paulie was in charge."

"He's your second-in-command?"

"This time. I rotate. Keeps things fair."

"Any chance whatever this thing is might've taken Ashley?"

"Taken her? Doubt it. Eaten her more likely. This thing is an opportunistic predator. Pretty sure it ate Officer Lindley last month, although Chief Garcia will tell you it was a rabid dog or some such nonsense."

"She mentioned there was blood but no body."

"It was unfortunate. We liked Officer Lindley." He turned to take in the view of downtown Fairhaven. "This is something else. You must feel like a princess in a tower up here."

I drank the water. "I have never once in my life felt like a princess."

"Sorry, should I have said queen?"

"That isn't what I meant. Besides, queens don't get locked in towers."

"No, I guess they don't." He tapped the outside of the empty glass in a mindless gesture.

"Do you like it here?" I asked. I wasn't sure where the question came from; it bubbled to the surface and popped out of my mouth before I could stop it.

"Love it. Wouldn't live anywhere else."

"Have you?" I asked. "Lived anywhere else?"

"I wasn't born here, if that's what you're asking."

"You joined the pack and became its alpha?" I whistled. "There's a story in there."

"One for another time." His gaze drifted back to the view. "If she isn't your friend, then what's your interest in Ashley Pratt?"

"Personally, none, but her brother offered to fix my computer if I located her. Seems like a fair deal."

West chuckled. "Something of a Luddite, are you?"

"I've learned a lot of skills over the years, but fixing a technology problem isn't one of them."

He pointed a finger at me. "Careful. Now I know your weakness."

"Feel free to exploit it." I envisioned my Amazon packages going to the wrong address in the future.

"Got any of Ashley's belongings?"

"A bracelet." I retrieved it from my pocket. I'd been carrying it around like a lucky charm. "Don't break it. It's meaningful to the girl."

West dangled the bracelet in front of him. "The kind of thing she wouldn't want to leave behind if she were to run away."

"Exactly."

"Have you tried a locator spell?" He tucked the bracelet into the front pocket of his jeans. They were so tight, I wasn't sure there was room for anything else.

"Yes. Didn't get anything."

"Fae or witch?"

"Witch. I find fae magic less reliable when it comes to locator spells."

He nodded. "Agreed. I'll send my trackers out tonight and report back to you."

"Thank you." I paused. "You don't want anything in return?"

West cleared his throat. "I'll be honest, Miss Clay."

"Lorelei."

"I'll be honest, Lorelei. Your presence here is a problem."

"Why is that?"

"Whatever you are, you're powerful. There's no use denying it. You had two of my wolves on the ground crying like babies without touching them. I can sense you the way I can sense a storm brewing. You're going to upset the balance in Fairhaven. There's a natural order of things, and you've gone and messed it up."

"Sounds like whatever is eating local cops has already upset the balance."

He met my gaze. "How do I know that something isn't you?"

I blew the air from nostrils. I wasn't about to put myself on trial. "I have no desire to upset anything. I plan to live in this heap of blue rubble and keep to myself."

"But you've already strayed from that plan, wouldn't you agree? You're demanding trackers."

"I'm not demanding."

"Doesn't matter. You asked, and I suspect I'd be a fool to deny your request. That's why I didn't ask for anything in return."

An uncomfortable knot formed in my chest. "This is why I prefer solitude."

"Have you considered the mountains?"

"The Poconos don't count?"

"There are more remote places."

I cocked an eyebrow. "Is that a suggestion?"

"No, ma'am. Wouldn't dream of it." He held up the empty glass. "I'll put this in the sink on my way out."

"Thank you."

I remained on the balcony, gazing at the horizon. I watched West exit the house. He didn't look up as he crossed the bridge, not that I expected him to. He passed through the gate, and turned in the direction of the woods, where I assumed he'd shift to run home.

"Do you think the wolves will find her?" Nana Pratt asked.

I hadn't realized she'd joined me on the balcony. "I don't know."

"He didn't seem to like you very much. Why not?"

"Because he's right about me. I upset the balance. They have a nice thing going here, and I could ruin it."

"I don't understand."

I looked at the old woman. "It's best if you don't." I left the balcony without another word.

CHAPTER 12

A Visconti isn't the only one who keeps his word. As promised, I returned to Otto's house to pay the vampire a social call, although my primary motivation was to find out whether he had any news about Ashley.

The housekeeper was friendlier when she answered the door, even greeting me by name. She escorted me to the same room as my last visit. This time, however, a chess set awaited me, as well as a buffet table laden with platters of food. Otto sat at the table with the chess set on the side with the black pieces.

"Are you expecting a small army?" I asked.

"I wasn't sure of your preferences, so I requested a smorgasbord."

"Well, you definitely got one." I plucked a purple grape from the bunch and ate it.

"I thought we might play chess while I share what my inquiries yielded."

"I'm not very good at chess. I'm more of a checkers girl."

"Then I'll teach you."

"I thought you were going to play the piano for me."

"Not to worry, I will. I've prepared my selections in advance."

"I expected nothing less." I heaped food on my plate, fully intending to return for a slice of chocolate cake.

"This board will be slightly different from what you're accustomed to," he explained.

"I told you; I'm not accustomed to any chessboards." I sat opposite him and studied the board, which had been adapted to accommodate his blindness. "The white squares are raised."

"Very good. And the black squares are sunken. See? You're already learning."

"And what did you learn about the trafficking claims?" I asked, diving right in.

"I spoke to three credible sources, and each one expressed bafflement. They were curious as to the origin of the claim."

"I've heard it from multiple camps now."

"Interesting. There've been no recent disagreements between the vampires and other groups, so it doesn't seem to be a retaliatory act."

"It could just be one of those rumors that takes on a life of its own." I'd endured more than one of those during my years in school.

"I don't know. The grapevine in Fairhaven tends to be surprisingly accurate." He offered a brief overview of the game. "If you have any questions as we play, don't hesitate to ask."

I tried to strategize and follow the rules, but my mind kept pulling me back to Ashley. Otto's repeated suggestions went in one ear and out the other.

"I'm sorry I'm not very good company," I said.

"It is interesting."

I leaned against the back of my chair. "Why interesting?"

"I wouldn't expect you to be so involved. It's one thing to strike a bargain, but I get the distinct sense that you care."

"I care about falling down on the job. I told Steven I'd help him. If Ashley dies, then I haven't held up my end of the bargain."

"From what I understand, you didn't promise to save her. You promised to help him find her. The two are not the same."

"But they're not mutually exclusive either." I moved my hand toward the board, but Otto waved it away. His vampire senses were finely attuned to movement.

"We'll keep the pieces where they are for next time," he said.

"We don't start over?"

He smirked. "Have you truly never played chess before?"

"I wasn't exaggerating. I'd rather hear you play, if you don't mind." I finished every crumb on my plate and returned to the buffet table for dessert. "Are you sure you don't want anything? It's all delicious."

"I have no doubt. Only the best for Otto Visconti and his guests."

As much as I loathed the word 'moist,' there was no better description for the cake. The frosting was the perfect blend of rich and sweet. I was tempted to ask for the recipe, but I knew myself too well to think I'd ever bake a cake, especially not now with so many projects in full swing.

Otto switched to the piano. I immediately recognized Clair de Lune; it was one of my favorites. The song ended, and Otto remained seated. "I played this for Anya once. I think Debussy bored her."

"It's beautiful." Debussy reminded me of my grandmother. I'd inherited my love of music from her. According to her, my parents had loved music, too. I'd been too young when they died to remember.

He motioned to the keys. "You're welcome to play next."

"Thank you, but no."

"You can certainly fit a piano in the Castle. It would be simple enough to find a secondhand one that needs a home."

"I wouldn't want to install a piano until I've finished painting," I said. It was a true statement that kept him from probing further.

"Would you sing for me?" Otto asked.

"Sorry, no."

"A pity. I sound like a jackhammer on a city street. It would be a nice change to hear someone else."

"That's what your playlist is for."

He smiled, and I caught a glimpse of his fangs. They were slightly stunted, like the rest of him.

The vibration of my phone against my hip startled me. I intended to reject the call until I saw Steven's name. Instead, I jumped to my feet. "Excuse me, Otto. I need to take this." I hurried into the corridor. "Lorelei Clay."

"Lorelei, it's Steven." The tremble in his voice unnerved me; if this was an Ashley update, I wasn't prepared.

"What's wrong?"

"I got a call from someone who says he knows where Ashley is."

"A Good Samaritan?"

"Do they count as a Good Samaritan if they demand money in exchange for the information?"

No, they definitely did not. "How much?"

"More than I have. Much more."

I sighed. "Did they offer any evidence that the information is accurate?"

"Should I have asked? I was so thrown by the call, I didn't really have time to think."

"What did you tell him?"

"That I'd give him whatever he wanted if he knew where I could find my sister."

My chest tightened; Steven was a devoted brother. Despite her predicament, I was envious of Ashley for having someone who cared about her as much as Steven did.

"Did he tell you where to bring the money?"

"He wants to meet at midnight at the Knob."

"Is that a bar?"

Steven snorted. "No, it's part of a hiking trail where you get a scenic overlook. It's out past Monk's and the pet resort."

"In other words, it's dark and isolated."

Steven was quiet for a moment. "It's worth it if I get her back. She's the only family I have." He hesitated. "The only living family."

I understood more than he knew. "I'll go with you."

He released a breath. "I was hoping you'd say that."

"But don't bring any money."

"What? How can I not bring the money?"

"Because if they really know where she is, then they're probably the ones who kidnapped her in the first place."

"Then they're dangerous, right? We should give them what they want."

"I'll give them a gift instead. Don't worry; they'll thank me for it." Okay, the latter part was a lie, but I hoped to reassure him.

"Should I pick you up?"

"No, meet me at my house. We'll take my motorcycle."

"You can't take motorized vehicles on the trail. People get in trouble for riding ATVs through there all the time."

"I don't think we're going to get a ticket, Steven. Live a little." We couldn't approach on foot, not when I had no idea who would be waiting for us at the end of the trail. There could be unscrupulous werewolves who could easily outrun us. I couldn't take the chance.

I tucked my phone in my pocket and returned to the room. "I assume you heard all that. My part, at least."

"Both parts." He tapped his ear. "Vampire hearing, remember?"

"Any thoughts?"

"Why would they wait so long to demand a ransom?"

"Agreed. It doesn't bode well."

"Bring a weapon. If you intend to ride a motorcycle, I'd park it a fair distance from the meeting point." He tapped his ear again and repeated, "Vampire hearing."

"Do you think vampires might have made the call?"

"This is Fairhaven, Miss Clay. Any number of supernaturals could be behind the call, and many of them have exceptional hearing."

"I'll keep it mind, thanks. Compliments to the chef on the food. Everything was incredible. Thank you for your hospitality."

"My pleasure, Miss Clay. Before you go, will you tell me who you are?"

"Clark Kent."

His sigh was tinged with disappointment. "Same time next week?"

I swung my purse over my shoulder. "A promise is a promise."

CHAPTER 13

I drove home from Walden Street deep in thought. Otto was right; the caller could be any number of supernaturals. It was possible Steven and I were in over our heads. Then again, I couldn't think of anyone better equipped to accompany Steven. Chief Garcia would be useless against most supernaturals.

I spotted Nana Pratt on the bridge as I passed through the gate.

"Lorelei, thank goodness you're back." She wrung her hands, inasmuch as a ghost could.

"What's wrong?"

"Come and see." She guided me to the cemetery where I stared at the upturned ground.

"What happened?" It looked like someone tried to dig up the plots. "Grave robbers?"

"Worse." Nana Pratt was so distraught, she could barely string words together.

Ray materialized beside her. "Whoever it was, they tried to get rid of us."

I blanched. "They tried to exorcise you?"

Nana Pratt seemed to recover her voice. "Why would I need that? I'm a ghost and a very trim one at that." She patted her hips.

"Not exercise. *Exorcise*. Cast you out of the cemetery."

Gasping, Nana reeled back. "They tried to kill us?"

"You're already dead," I reminded her.

"Then why are we still here?" Ray asked.

"Because they don't know what they're doing. Did you recognize anyone?"

"No," she said. "They wore black hoods like the intruder."

"How many of them?"

"Three this time," Ray said.

"Could you tell if they were men or women?" I asked.

They shook their heads in unison.

"They held hands and chanted," Nana Pratt recounted, "but their voices were too low to tell."

Chanting in a cemetery could be anybody. Even vampires could perform a ritual with the right tools. It was their goal I was interested in—why cast out the spirits? What did they hope to gain from that?

"Why didn't you get a closer look?" I asked.

"Because I didn't want them to catch me." Nana said this like it was the most obvious reason in the world.

I pondered the mess. "It's a cemetery, and the only one who'd be inconvenienced by the ghosts here is me."

"Maybe someone was trying to do you a favor," Ray offered.

"Doubtful."

"You didn't sense anybody breaching the ward?" Ray asked.

"No, it only works when I'm on the property."

"Maybe they ought to fix that," he said.

"What's the point?" Nana shot back. "If she isn't here, there isn't much she can do, is there?"

"Well, she'd know to hurry home. It was awful to watch them and not be able to contact you." Ray seemed genuinely distressed, and I felt a pang of sympathy for him.

"Help me," a timid voice called. "Please, help me."

I turned toward the gate to see a young woman stumbling forward. My body reacted as she crossed the ward. Her hair was matted to her head, and there were bloodstains on her clothes. For a fleeting moment, I thought she might be Ashley, except this girl had reddish-brown hair. I tried to disguise my disappointment.

I rushed forward and met her halfway. She fell to her knees, sobbing.

"I don't know her," Nana Pratt said.

"Me neither," Ray said.

I kept my focus on the girl. "Where are you hurt?"

The girl continued to cry.

"Poor dear," Nana Pratt said. "She's too upset to talk. I recall a similar experience."

Ray looked at her. "You were attacked and ran to the nearest house?"

"No, I'd lost the promise ring that my Edward had given me. I was beside myself. Couldn't form words I cried so hard."

"Yes, that's the same," Ray remarked wryly.

"Let's get you inside." I slipped my arm behind the girl and helped her to her feet.

She whimpered as she straightened her legs, and I wondered whether any bones were fractured. She seemed able to walk albeit with a slight limp. She was a human, so I wasn't about to call for a fae healer.

I guided her into the house to the kitchen, mainly because it was the only room with chairs. If I could get her comfortable and talking, maybe she knew something about Ashley.

"You need a couch like a normal person," Nana Pratt said.

"Criticize her later," Ray scolded. "She's busy."

"I don't want to ruin your chair," the girl whispered. "I'm a mess."

"Nothing is precious here," I promised. "Sit. I'll get you a glass of water."

"Thank you." Her voice sounded hoarse, from screaming or crying, I wasn't sure.

I filled a glass and set it on the table next to her. "What's your name?"

"Lyra."

"Well, Lyra, today's your lucky day. I have a First Aid kit and plenty of bandages. I don't want to overstep, but if you tell me more about your injuries, I can help."

She studied me with interest. "Are you a doctor?"

"No, but I had a grandfather who disliked them, so he taught me how to do basic medical care." It wasn't a lie. My grandfather avoided most professionals and authority figures. His distrust of 'the system' ran deep. He taught me how to suture and dress wounds before I was twelve. He wasn't particularly clumsy, but he was constantly in need of a bandage or an ice pack. The older he got, the worse his injuries.

The girl kicked off her flip-flop and stuck out her leg. A bright red gash slanted across her skin.

"How many more of those do you have?"

She lifted the hem of her shirt to reveal a cut across her abdomen.

"Animal attack?" I queried.

She nodded. "It was big. I think it was a giant bear. I was so shocked, all I could think about was getting away."

"Well, you managed that part well enough. What were you doing in the woods?"

"Hiking."

"Alone and in those shoes?" I squinted at her. "What were you really doing there?"

She lowered her gaze to the floor. "I was supposed to meet this guy I met online, but he didn't show. I waited an hour past the time he said in case he was running late. I just decided to leave when I got attacked."

"How did you get away?" Bears were faster than most people believed.

"I ran as fast as I could. I picked up a log and threw it behind me. Maybe I hit it or scared it off. I didn't stop to look." Tears filled her eyes again. "I almost died."

"But you didn't. Got a number for this guy you were supposed to meet?" Maybe this was connected to Ashley after all.

She seemed momentarily dazed. After snapping to attention, she pulled her phone from her pocket and opened an app to show me. "His name is Theo."

"Or that's what he said his name is. Why did he want to meet in the woods?" And why would this girl think it was a smart idea?

"He was very romantic. He talked about these nature poets like Walden and Thoreau. I thought if he liked poetry, that was a good sign."

"Serial killers can like poetry," I pointed out.

Nana Pratt gasped. "Lorelei, this young woman is traumatized. Less judgment and more compassion, please."

I changed tacks. "Where do you live, Lyra?"

"She isn't local," Nana Pratt said. "I'd know her face."

"Outside Port Jervis. I took the bus to Fairhaven and walked the rest of the way."

Nana Pratt crossed her arms, satisfied. "See? Told you."

"Do you live with your parents?"

Her face paled. "Please don't call them. My dad is so strict. He'll punish me for the rest of my life if he finds out I went to meet a strange man in the woods."

"Maybe a little punishment isn't such a bad idea. Might teach you a lesson."

She gestured to her wounds. "You think this isn't punishment enough?"

"You're going to need to make sure these wounds don't get infected. I don't know how you'll manage without telling your parents. They'll want you to see a doctor."

"They won't take me anywhere. We don't have health insurance," she admitted.

I understood that all too well.

I'd have to mention the animal attack to the chief. She might want to speak to Lyra.

"Why don't you give me your number?"

Lyra fixed me with a wary eye. "Why?"

"There've been a rash of animal attacks lately. The chief of police is looking into them. She may want to talk to you."

Lyra gave her head a hard shake. "No way. If my parents find out the chief of police wants to speak to me, that's a big red flag. Huge."

I sighed. I couldn't force her to share personal information with me, as much as I wanted to. She was alive, for one thing; I had no control over the living.

"Promise me you'll not try to meet any more strangers over the Internet, and that you'll take care of those cuts."

"I swear!" She practically jumped out of the chair. "I'm such an idiot. He was so nice though." Biting her lip, she looked at me. "I feel like there's something you're not telling me."

"I told you about the animal attacks."

"No, I feel like you might know something about this guy. Have there been other girls like me?"

I debated whether to share information about Ashley. In the end, I figured it couldn't hurt. "There's a missing young woman named Ashley Pratt."

"My grandbaby," Nana Pratt chimed in.

Lyra's face was solemn. "Do you think she might've been meeting the same guy?"

"I didn't know about him until now, but it seems like a thread worth tugging."

"What did you think happened to her before now?"

"The police think she ran away. Had a fight with her brother and took off. They think she'll come back once she's calmed down or runs out of money."

"But you don't think that," she said, more of a statement than a question.

"No. I don't." I swiped her empty glass off the table and placed it in the sink. "I traced her to a clearing in Wild Acres." I drew the line at sharing the wolf pack's involvement. It was doubtful this girl knew anything about the supernatural world. She seemed to be in denial about the creature that attacked her. I'd bet good money those weren't marks from a bear.

"And then what?" Lyra prompted.

"It's like she vanished into thin air."

"Maybe the police are right and she ran away. I had a friend who did that. I think about it, too, sometimes."

"How old are you?"

"Seventeen."

"One more year then. You can do it."

Lyra placed a hand on the top of the chair to steady herself. "Thanks for the help. I'm so glad I found this place. I ran and ran. I had no clue where I was going; I was just so desperate to get away."

"Adrenaline is our friend in those situations."

"Tell her you'll drive her to the town line, so no one sees you," Ray suggested.

I scowled at Ray. I didn't want to drive anybody anywhere. I wanted to clean up the mess that the intruders had made in the cemetery and get on with my day.

Ray noticed my expression because he said, "What? She's hurt. You can't make her walk, even to the bus stop. It's uncivilized."

I counted to five in my head. "Lyra, how about I drive you close to Port Jervis and then you can hobble the rest of the way."

Lyra considered the offer. "Okay."

The drive took twenty minutes. Lyra was silent most of the way, only speaking to offer directions and to ask me the occasional question about myself, to which I gave my usual vague answers.

"You seem different," Lyra said, scrutinizing me from the passenger seat.

"I lived abroad for a few years. It changes a person."

"Wow, another country. That's so cool. I've always wanted to travel. Where'd you live?"

"London, most recently."

"Guess you didn't like it much."

Perceptive girl. "What makes you say that?"

"Because you moved here. I don't know why anybody would choose Fairhaven over a city as cool as London though."

"London has its charms."

"Well, your town doesn't have any. Neither does mine." She seemed to notice our location. "Here's good," she said.

I pulled to the shoulder of the road and let the engine idle. "Take care of yourself, Lyra."

"I will, thanks." She jumped to the ground and hobbled away.

I put the truck in reverse and drove home. That was my good deed for the day. I hoped I wouldn't encounter any more bloody girls on the route home because they'd be shit out of luck.

I spent the remainder of the day painting the front room and trying not to dwell on my evening plans. A text from Steven confirmed he'd arrive at the Castle at eleven-thirty, which dragged my mind back to the mystery meetup.

By the time I finished painting, my arms were sore, and my clothes were splattered with eggshell paint. I ate an apple with almond butter for dinner, still full from Otto's spread, and went upstairs to my bedroom to change.

I opted for a dark green top and black shorts.

"I don't like the idea of my Steven confronting a bunch of thugs," Nana Pratt said, pacing the area at the foot of my bed.

"And I don't like the idea of ghosts violating the boundaries I've clearly set." I tossed her an annoyed look as I placed my dirty clothes in the hamper.

"You weren't doing anything interesting," Nana said.

"I changed my clothes."

"Nothing I haven't seen before. I have all the same parts."

I swiveled to face her. "It doesn't matter. What matters is this is my sanctuary, and you've entered it without permission. It can't happen again." I gave her a pointed look. "Do you understand?"

She pointed at my phone on the bed. "That's my grandson…"

"I don't care if it's the leader of an alien race giving me a heads-up that they're about to take over the planet. It's not your business. How would you feel if some stranger was watching Ashley get undressed?"

"When you put it that way…" Nana lowered her head, presumably in shame. It was hard to tell. "I apologize, Lorelei. I was only thinking about myself. You have to understand, though. Steven and Ashley only have each other. I can't bear the thought of something bad happening to either one of them."

"I do understand," I said, "and I'm doing my best to help them, but that doesn't give you the right to repeatedly violate my boundaries. Right now, I only intend to ward the property line, but that plan can change at any time." It would mean a return visit to the witches, which I didn't love, but I was willing to do whatever it took to preserve my peace. I didn't move all this way and uproot my life again to be nothing more than a ghost magnet. I should've forced Nana Pratt and Ray to cross over with the rest of the spirits.

Nana Pratt seemed to get the hint. Without another word, she disappeared.

At quarter past eleven, I went to the outbuilding I used to house Betsy, my motorcycle. She wasn't a new model by any stretch of the imagination, but she'd get the job done. I bought her years ago and left her in a storage unit with my other belongings when I left for England. She only needed a little love and care when I finally reclaimed her. My grandfather would often grumble about the quality of modern machines, and I'd mock his longing for 'the good, old days,' but I'd finally reached the point in life where I agreed with him.

I rifled through a cardboard box to find a second helmet for Steven. No sense risking a head injury. Ashley wouldn't want to be reunited with her brother in a hospital.

Steven arrived ten minutes later, and we set off for the Knob. I'd done my due diligence before we left so I knew where to go. The trail was only a mile and a half long. Halfway to the Knob, I killed the lights and the engine.

"What are you doing?" Steven whispered, unwrapping his arms from my waist.

"We're going the rest of the way on foot. I'll leave this hidden behind a tree." I scanned the silhouettes for the largest tree and rolled the bike over to it.

"Why?" Steven asked.

"Because I want them to think we trust them. If we show up on getaway wheels, they'll be suspicious that we intend to split fast."

Steven bit his lip as he glanced uneasily in the direction of the Knob. "Should we have brought a weapon?" He sounded mildly panicked.

"I came prepared. Don't forget the backpack."

He pivoted to the side to show me the blue sack strapped to his back.

"Great. Let's go."

We hiked the remainder of the trail to the Knob, which wasn't as easy as I anticipated. The trail climbed higher and higher, which I should've realized when Steven said the Knob was an overlook, but I'd been too distracted by the new development.

I listened to the soothing sounds of the forest as we walked along the trail. Entire worlds were housed in a single forest. My grandfather had taught me to pay attention to the noises and identify their sources. Bushes shook as tiny feet scampered away from us.

Up ahead I saw three man-shaped silhouettes. They stood so close together that they nearly formed a single black blob.

"Let me do the talking," I told Steven in a quiet voice.

He nodded wordlessly.

"Hey, there," I called. "I hope you're the guys we're meeting because this forest is giving me the creeps. I want nothing more than to go home and cuddle with Steven on the couch."

Steven shot me a quizzical look but said nothing.

The first man emerged from the shadows. Bald and stocky, he grinned like a car salesman about to sell us a lemon. That smile told me what I needed to know.

"As long as you brought the money, you can be back on your couch in fifteen minutes."

"Not if we have to stop to pick up Ashley on the way," I countered.

"Right, of course." He stroked the soul patch on his chin, a move that made me want to rip each hair out from its follicle one by one.

His two companions peeled away from the darkness to join him. Tall and muscular and...

"Twins?" I asked. "That's new."

Soul Patch squinted in disbelief. "You've never seen twins before?"

"I've never seen twins acting as the muscle. It's a fresh twist. I wholeheartedly approve."

The twins exchanged confused glances.

"Where's my sister?" Steven demanded.

Soul Patch wiggled his fingers. "The money first."

I positioned myself between them. "Not a chance. First, we need to know your information is good."

"We're not telling you anything until we count the money," Soul Patch said.

"Is that why you brought reinforcements? To help you count? I don't blame you; math was never my strong suit either."

He didn't seem to enjoy my sass. He shifted his attention to Steven. "If you want to see your little sister again, you'll shut your girlfriend's mouth."

"She's right, though. We need proof of life," Steven said. I was impressed by his ability to remain calm. I half worried he'd panic and run.

Laughing, Soul Patch looked at his companions. "Proof of life? This isn't a military extraction."

Steven's eyes blazed with anger. "Tell us where Ashley is, and you'll get your money."

"Nope. We're doing it my way, or no way at all."

They didn't know anything. I felt it in my gut the same way I felt the presence of restless spirits before I could see them. It had been my assumption from the start, but I knew I wouldn't be able to persuade Steven otherwise. Although he wouldn't get proof of life, I was about to give him proof of lies.

I took a step closer to them. "Fine, you win. Ashley is more important than losing this game you're forcing us to play." I held out my hand to Steven. "Backpack, please."

He slipped the straps off his shoulders and passed the bag to me. I offered the bag to Soul Patch. The moment his hand gripped one of the straps, I yanked the bag toward me, and Soul Patch with it. I kept one hand on the bag and wrapped my other arm around his shoulders. To the untrained eye, it looked like I was giving him an awkward hug.

The twins seemed uncertain how to react—until their companion started to scream and wriggle. That *might* have been a giveaway that I was giving him more than affection.

As his arms flailed in distress, I dragged Soul Patch backward, prompting the twins to advance. "Any closer and I'll make sure he stops screaming." I paused. "That's not actually a good thing." My skills weren't polished in the art of intimidation, not when it came to humans anyway. I actively avoided using my powers on them because it wasn't a fair fight.

The twins halted in their tracks. The one on the left angled his head for a better view. "What are you doing to him—pressing on a nerve?"

"That's one way of describing it." The brain was, after all, the hub of the nervous system. "Do you really know where Ashley is?"

Their guilty faces answered my question.

"This was about money?" Steven asked. His voice was a combination of shock and disappointment. Poor guy.

"It was his idea," the twin on the left motioned to Soul Patch. "He offered us a cut to come along with him and act intimidating."

"And you did a commendable job," I told them.

"I was intimidated," Steven admitted.

I released my hold on Soul Patch before I gave him permanent brain damage. He dropped to the ground and curled into the fetal position, mumbling softly to himself.

"Will he be okay?" the twin on the right asked.

"Give him a couple hours, and he'll be fine, but I'd advise

against watching any of the Halloween movies for at least two weeks."

The twins stared at me with matching expressions of confusion. I didn't bother to elaborate.

I turned to Steven. "Do you recognize any of those guys?"

He shook his head, visibly shaken by the experience. "They're not local."

I turned back to the trio. "How did you know about Ashley?"

The twin on the right nudged Soul Patch with his shoe. "A buddy of his. They were drinking at Monk's together, and he mentioned a girl had gone missing from there."

"And you all decided to prey on an innocent man and give him false hope? Do you now see how that isn't a decent thing to do?"

The twins' heads bobbed in unison.

"Don't contact Steven again," I warned, "or I will hunt the three of you down and, trust me, you won't like what I do to you."

I tossed the backpack to Steven and walked away. I heard his footsteps pounding the trail as he hurried after me.

"Are they following us?" I asked in a low voice.

Steven snuck a peak over his shoulder. "No, they're staring at the guy on the ground. They don't seem to know what to do."

"Good."

The sound of cicadas filled the air. They were louder than usual tonight. Trees rustled, and a flock of birds flew overhead, flapping their wings and squawking. I brushed off the unsettled feeling; it was probably my guilt over intimidating humans. I took no pleasure in it.

"What did you do to him?" Steven asked, once we were seated on the motorcycle.

"Nothing you need to worry about."

"You can do more than talk to ghosts, can't you?"

I revved the engine. "Let's pretend this never happened, and we'll both be happier, okay?"

Steven didn't argue. He held onto my waist as I turned the motorcycle in the direction of home.

CHAPTER 14

I opened the window in my bedroom and heard the sound of an owl hooting. The noise was reassuring somehow. I felt like I had a feathered sentry, much like the blackbird that seemed to gravitate to the gate. I got along with most animals, except dogs. My presence unsettled them. I had to steer clear, or they'd howl like mad, and in my experience, if people notice their dog doesn't like you, they don't like you either.

I tried to read *The Complete History of Fairhaven*, but I couldn't focus on the book. I even picked up *Pride & Prejudice* for the hundredth time but to no avail. My thoughts kept returning to Ashley. I wondered whether this Theo character might be connected to her disappearance. It was possible Theo was a vampire luring young women into the woods.

I tossed and turned in an effort to get comfortable. The heat and humidity refused to allow it. The fan wasn't much help. Its main function seemed to be blowing strands of my hair across my sweaty face so they stuck there.

I awoke to a prickling sensation all over my body. I sat up with a start when I realized the ward had been activated.

Throwing off the sheet, I bolted downstairs in the same T-shirt and shorts I'd slept in. Nobody would be the wiser.

I peered outside to see West's shadow pacing the length of my porch, rubbing the back of his neck. In the distance, the faint glow of sunrise was spreading across the horizon.

His head swung toward the door as it opened. "We've got a situation," he said with a grim expression. "Can you come?"

If I had been anybody else, he wouldn't have phrased it as a question. Whatever this was, it was unpleasant, and he was damn unhappy about it.

"Did you drive?"

He swore. "No, sorry. I came from the woods."

"We can take my truck." I hurried to the kitchen counter for my keys.

As I crossed the porch, Nana Pratt and Ray appeared.

"I wanted to tell you he was here," Nana Pratt said, "but Ray made me stay outside because of the rules."

"And Ray was right to do that."

His face turned smug, and she jerked her head away to avoid looking at him.

West was already waiting by the passenger door when I arrived outside. Despite the hour, the moon was still faintly visible, a gossamer disc in the sky. The werewolf remained in stoic silence for the duration of the drive, only choosing to speak to indicate where to turn. I arrived at the edge of the woods, near one of the hiking trails.

"This way," he said.

I parked the truck and followed him on foot through the forest. The distant sounds of the highway faded to silence. Moisture gathered on my upper lip; today promised to be a scorcher. Thankfully, the air cooled as we traveled into the heart of the forest, where the morning light waned, unable to break through the dense trees. The scent of fresh pine and rich soil gave way to earthy decay.

The forest was eerily quiet. No birdsong. No scampering

of tiny feet like last night. No cicadas to warn us of the unpleasant heat to come.

My skin prickled. I could feel the breath of death around us. I almost told him about last night's false lead, but I didn't want to disturb the quiet.

I wasn't surprised when West directed me to one of his pack members. He was face down on the ground, his wounds being tended by two more werewolves, male and female. His clothes were in shreds, and his body was covered in angry red slashes.

Another so-called animal attack. I wondered whether it was the same beast that attacked Lyra.

West looked down at them. "This is Arthur. He's one of my trackers."

I stared at Arthur's injured body. "He was tracking Ashley."

"He got separated from the others last night. They found him like this."

"He's still alive," I said. Barely.

West snuck a hopeful peek at me. "Can we keep it that way?"

"I don't have that kind of power, West. I'm sorry."

"Didn't think so but had to ask. Arthur's a good kid."

The two other werewolves turned to regard us. They seemed reluctant to stand, as though the mere change in position would cause Arthur to shake off his mortal coil.

"Nothing we do is working," the female said. "The wounds are too deep. He's lost a lot of blood."

"Keep applying pressure to the wounds, Magda," West ordered.

"You don't want to call the paramedics or take him to a hospital?" I asked.

West gazed at Arthur with a solemn expression. "Humans can't help him."

I contemplated the wounds. "How do you know for sure?"

"Because we fought the creature that attacked him," West said grimly.

"And you didn't mention that in the truck?"

He was unapologetic. "Didn't feel much like talking."

"Did you kill it?"

"No, it got away, but we managed to defang it, so it won't be biting anyone else anytime soon." West looked at his companions. "We'll assemble a team to hunt it down as soon as we can regroup."

"Did you keep the fangs?"

West snarled. "Do I look like the tooth furry to you? No, I didn't keep a souvenir."

"Do you know what it was?" I asked, adopting my most patient tone. Those fangs would've helped identify the creature if the werewolves couldn't.

"A big snake," Magda interrupted.

"That's an understatement," the other werewolf said. "It was monstrous." He wiped Arthur's brow. "His body is on fire."

Magda swallowed a cry. "It must be poison."

"Seems likely," West said. "Without knowing more, we can't help him."

"What about Sage?" Magda asked.

West perked up. "That's a good idea."

"I don't think sage will help in a situation like this," I said.

"She will if we pay her," the other werewolf said. He still hadn't been referred to by name, and it didn't seem like the right time to ask for an introduction.

"Sage is one of the fair folk," West explained.

"Destiny Woods isn't far from here." Magda slid her arms underneath Arthur's shoulders. "We should hurry."

West crouched beside Arthur. "Let me."

Magda backed away and let the alpha carry Arthur. West

was strong, no doubt about it. He lifted Arthur like he weighed no more than a plank of wood.

I trailed after them to a red cabin nestled in a clearing. There were a few other cabins within view, but they were far enough away to afford this one privacy.

The front door flew open as though the occupant was expecting us. We must've tripped a ward on the way here.

"Sage, we need help," West called.

A woman emerged from the cabin in a T-shirt, shorts, and bare feet. Her unkempt blonde hair was streaked, and her face was round and cheerful, the kind of youthful face that made it difficult to guess her age. She took one look at Arthur in West's arms and motioned them inside.

"What happened?" she asked, still groggy from sleep.

"An attack." West carried the limp werewolf across the threshold and into the cabin. The interior was surprisingly bright for a cabin in the woods. Every surface gleamed like it had been scrubbed by a small army.

Sage guided them to an adjacent room where a long table took center stage. West set Arthur down and backed away to give her space, bumping into a row of jars in the process. He quickly straightened them.

Her gaze flicked to me. "I don't know you."

"Lorelei Clay."

"I'm Sage; it's short for Savage."

"It is not," a voice croaked from another room. "You were named after the herb."

"Hush, Gran. This doesn't concern you." She rubbed her hands together and placed them on Arthur's body. "He's fighting an infection. Was whatever attacked him poisonous?"

"The fangs might've been venomous," I said.

"What's the difference?" Magda asked.

"It's considered poisonous if you inhale or swallow the toxin, or it's absorbed by the skin. It's venomous if it's injected," I explained.

"Seems like a minor distinction," West said.

"Not if you're the one dying from it," I remarked.

Sage examined the wounds. "You don't know the type of creature that did this?"

"A big snake," Magda said. "Huge."

"Supernatural," West added.

Sage opened Arthur's shirt and inspected the marks. "They're bright red." She turned away from Arthur and began to collect materials. She sniffed a jar and quickly put it back. "I need to restock that one."

"Try the poultice I made last week for Maisie," Gran yelled.

"No back seat healing," Sage shouted. She bit her lower lip in concentration. "That won't work. Let me try another combo." Her hands moved so swiftly that they blurred.

"Smells like burnt coffee," Magda observed.

"I don't care if smells like sulphur and acid, as long as it saves Arthur," West said.

Sage applied the mixture to the wounds. Arthur remained motionless. Even his soft moans had stopped.

"I'm sorry," Sage finally said. "Nothing's working."

"We should take him back to Arrowhead," Magda said. "At least let him die comfortably in his bed."

"He's a wolf," West said. "We'll take him outside. If he's going to die, let it be in the place that's brought him the most joy."

A shriek pierced the quiet of the forest. The alpha's body reacted instinctively; he seemed on the verge of shifting.

Their companion shot to the nearest window. "What in the hell was that?"

A wailing cry followed the shriek. Inwardly I groaned. "Wait here. I'll take care of it."

"I'll come with you," West said, starting forward.

I held up a hand. "Trust me. You don't want to see this."

West shot me a quizzical look as I exited the cabin. I

threaded my way through the trees, following the horrific sound until I found her in the midst of one of her infamous cries. "Fy mlentyn! Fy mlentyn bach!"

"He isn't a child," I said.

The hideous figure stopped wailing and fixed me with black, pupilless eyes that looked even more striking amidst the backdrop of her pallid complexion. Her long black hair was tangled in knots. Skeletal arms poked out from the short sleeves of her full-length shift dress. Black wings that resembled the sails of a ship protruded from her back.

The hideous figure gasped. "You're here. 'Tis true."

"'Tis. What are you doing here, Gwen?" Similar to an Irish banshee, Gwen was a harbinger of doom, a terrifying Welsh spirit whose sole purpose was to warn others of imminent death. Gwrach y Rhibyn she was once called—the Witch of Rhibyn.

"I think you know why." Gwen opened her mouth, revealing a set of black teeth, and resumed her horrible shrieks.

I rolled my eyes. "We get it, Gwen. He's dying. No need for musical accompaniment. Move along."

The harbinger glowered at me. "You don't see me interfering with your role. Let me do my job."

"This one is off limits."

Gwen licked her bloodstained lips. "You cannot prevent death, f'anwylyd. You know that better than most."

"I'm not trying to prevent death. I'm trying to preserve his dignity."

Gwen gathered the material of her dress in her hands. "I have no idea what you mean. I gather here to sound the trumpet."

"You gather here to drink his blood knowing he's about to die."

She waved a dismissive hand. "Bah! Old wives' tales. You

know me better than that." She advanced toward the cabin. "Let me pass. I have a job to do."

I moved to block her path. "Pennsylvania is nowhere near Wales. What are you even doing here?"

"I'm a traveling spirit now. I grew weary of wailing in one place."

"I don't think this town needs you. It seems to have plenty of supernatural activity."

"All the more reason to stay."

"No, absolutely not. I forbid it."

Gwen drew back; her eyes sparked with anger. "You dare command me?"

Folding my arms, I leveled her with a look. "I dare."

She blew a raspberry. "Fine. Keep your Falls to yourself."

"Falls?"

"Water that cascades from the side of a cliff. You know. A waterfall."

I heaved an irritated sigh. "I know what a waterfall is. What are you talking about?"

"The Falls in your Wild Acres is acting as a conductor and generating powerful magical energy."

Huh. I learned something new every day. "Is that what brought you here?"

"No. I heard you were here."

Of course. "You spoke to Matilda."

"We ran into each other at a funeral. She told me how to find you."

I'd be sure to thank her later. "Listen, I appreciate that you came to check on me, but why don't you leave this one to me?"

She recoiled, affronted. "I have dibs. He was killed by one of mine."

I frowned. "One of yours?"

"A gwiber is a beast of Wales."

The 'big snake' was a gwiber. Of course. "Then how did it get here?"

"No idea, cariad. Possibly the same way I did, the crossroads."

I debated my options. I didn't want to insult Gwen, but I couldn't let her abuse the dying werewolf. "I'd consider it a very great favor if you let me handle this one."

She peered past me, as though she could glimpse her target from here. "Did you know him?"

"Not really, but I live here now. I want to get along with people."

"He's not a person. He's a werewolf."

"Fine. I want to get along with everyone. Is that better?"

She squinted, skeptical. "You don't normally like to mix with others. What's changed, cariad?"

"Nothing. I don't want to mix with them. I only want to stay in one place, and that requires not making trouble for myself." A concept the Welsh spirit wouldn't understand.

Gwen's gaze slid past me. "Very well then. He's all yours."

"Thank you."

"When am I permitted to visit?"

"We'll put something on the calendar once my house is ready for company." In about five more years.

Appeased, she raised her arms and spread her wings in preparation for a dramatic exit.

"You don't have to do that with me. I know you."

Gwen paused, leaving her bony arms outstretched. "It's part of my routine. It won't feel right if I don't do it."

"You do you then, boo."

Her wings flapped in the breeze and smacked against the surrounding tree trunks. "Ugh," she groaned; her arms collapsed at her sides. "This forest is too dense to fly."

"Tell that to the birds."

The harbinger raised her arms again and disappeared

behind a cloud of black smoke. Coughing, I waved my hand in front of my face to disperse the debris she'd stirred. I heard the crunch of her footsteps as she ran through the forest in the opposite direction.

Once the air settled, I noticed Arthur in an upright position. He stared at me with soulful brown eyes.

"Thank you for not letting the spirit defile my body," he said.

"A gwiber did this to you?"

His brown eyes rounded. "It was a nightmare come true."

"Everyone feels that way about death."

"No, not death. The creature that served it to me. My grandmother used to tell me stories about the gwiber as a child. They terrified me."

"Your grandmother was a member of the Arrowhead pack?"

"She moved here from Wales as a young girl and married my grandfather. He was already a member."

"Do you remember the details of the attack?"

"I was following a scent, and the gwiber crossed my path. I couldn't believe it was real. My hesitation cost me my life." He craned his neck to look in the direction of the cabin. "What happens now?"

"I can help you cross over, if that's your preference."

He nodded. "It is. I'd like to join the rest of my family." He fixed me with shining eyes. "Will it hurt?"

"Not anymore." I held up my hand. "Continue your journey, Arthur. Be at peace."

Arthur looked at me skeptically. "That's it?"

"It's only complicated if you make it so."

His form dissipated.

I emerged from the trees and returned to the cabin; my footsteps now heavier than when I left.

"Arthur's gone," West said, "but I guess you already knew that."

Sage grew alert. "You speak to spirits?"

"Who speaks to spirits?" Gran demanded from the other room.

"None of your business, Gran! Go back to sleep."

"How can I sleep with werewolves dying on my table?" the old woman called.

Sage rolled her eyes.

"He was killed by a gwiber."

West glanced at his companions. "Anybody know what that is?"

They shook their heads.

"I guess the animal attack rumor isn't as far-fetched as we believed," West remarked.

I remembered the cop whose body hadn't been found. "There was a cop killed last month, presumably another animal attack. They found her blood but not her body."

"So?" Sage said.

"So, the gwiber is a giant snake. It probably ate the cop whole."

"It would've swallowed Arthur whole, too, if we hadn't interrupted it," West said.

"A lot of animals have gone missing the past couple months," Sage said. "A giant snake monster would explain it."

"If it's that big, how has no one spotted it?" the nameless werewolf asked.

"Good question, Kurt," West said.

Kurt. Got it.

I looked at Sage. "What kind of animals?"

"All different sorts. Livestock. Bloodhounds. Even my friend's cat."

"We don't know the giant snake is responsible for all that," Kurt said. "Maybe it's a coincidence."

"You'd think the deer would keep the creature well fed,"

Magda said. "We've got more than our share of them in these woods."

West observed Arthur's body. "I don't care about the damn goats and chickens. I care that we just lost one of our own."

"I understand, West," Magda said quietly, "but know thy enemy, right? If it doesn't eat deer, maybe there's a reason."

"Maybe it doesn't like the taste of venison. I don't really give a shit." West clenched his fists. "The only thing I want to know right now is how to kill it."

CHAPTER 15

It bothered me that the monster that killed Arthur was one whose stories had tormented him as a child. If his nightmare had come true, I worried that I was somehow to blame, except I'd used my powers very sparingly since my arrival, and I hadn't spent time in Arthur's head. And how did the gwiber relate to Ashley's disappearance? I couldn't connect the dots.

Of course, there was always a chance it was a coincidence that a gwiber of all things had killed him. People sometimes attracted the thing they feared most. The universe had a twisted sense of humor.

If the pack was going to hunt the gwiber, the least I could do was offer information that might help their search. Without decent Internet service, I had no choice but to use the public computer at the library to conduct my research. The Internet on my phone was too unreliable. I'd get halfway through an article and lose connection. It made me twitchy to read too much on my phone anyway; the screen was too small.

The library parking lot was surprisingly crowded. I couldn't imagine what had attracted so many people at once.

I spotted Hailey crossing the parking lot from a different angle and waved. We met on the corner of the sidewalk.

"How's that James Patterson book?"

"It isn't due back yet, is it?" It would take time for Ray to finish the book. He complained that he hadn't yet mastered turning the pages. I told him that it would take practice. He seemed to think that because he'd thrown wooden boards around that he could do anything now. It was the difference between bludgeoning someone and performing open heart surgery.

"Not yet," Hailey said, "and you can always renew it if you need to."

"Is this a typical Thursday?" I asked, gesturing to the cars.

"Toddler story hour. Fair warning, it's a little on the noisy side. They don't tend to grasp the concept of quiet time at this age."

I'd have to persevere. I needed the information more than I needed quiet time. As I was about to respond, a figure caught my eye as she emerged from the library. She wore a black dress that reached her ankles, along with black laced boots.

"Hey, Vic." Hailey waved to the woman she passed.

The woman smiled in greeting and continued toward downtown on foot.

"You can see her?" I whispered.

Hailey's brow creased. "Of course I can see her."

"What's her story? Why the library?" There'd been a few ghosts I regularly encountered in the London Library, but not as many I would've expected in a city as old as London.

Hailey seemed confused by the question. "She's twenty-two, I think. Moved here last year after she graduated college. Her real name is Sasha, but everyone calls her Vic because of the Victorian dresses she wears. Doesn't matter what the weather is; she's always dressed like that. I'd sweat my ass off, but Vic doesn't seem bothered."

It took me a moment to process that Vic wasn't a ghost. "She dresses like a Victorian woman. Why?"

"Who knows? I thought it was odd at first, but now I think it's kind of cool." Hailey laughed. "Why would you think I couldn't see her? I mean, she does blend in at nighttime. Once the sun sets, she has that Cheshire cat thing where you can't see her until she smiles."

Hailey advanced toward the entrance, and I fell in step with her. "There definitely seems to be an eclectic crowd in Fairhaven."

"One of the many reasons I love it. Wait until you meet the Kangs. They have a whole fleet of cars. Don't let them corner you, or you'll be stuck looking at their five thousand photos. They show off pictures of their cars the way other people show off their kids or pets."

No doubt the Kangs were friendly with Otto.

We entered the library where Hailey was immediately engulfed by patrons. I cut straight through the crowd and headed to the cluster of computers.

I became so engrossed in my research that I lost track of time. Hailey's voice cut through my concentration. "Whatcha working on?" She leaned over my shoulder. "Ooh, mythological creatures. I love those. What's a gwiber?"

I shushed her. "Aren't we supposed to keep our voices down in the library?"

Hailey gave me a pointed look. "I told you about toddler time."

I peered over the top of the computer. Sure enough, the other side of the room was teeming with boisterous children. Their adult supervisors seemed to have given up on keeping their charges quiet.

"Tell me about the gwiber. I love learning new things."

Probably why she was good at her job. "It's a snake monster, Welsh in origin."

"I have a whole section on mythology that might help

you. Why don't we bypass Mr. Wikipedia and friends, and check with our old friend, Dewey Decimal?"

Warmth flooded my cheeks. It suddenly seemed like sacrilege to be conducting an Internet search in a library. Then again, I was in a hurry and assumed the Internet would be faster. My mistake.

"That would be great," I said. "Do I need to switch to a different screen?"

"No need when you've got the librarian as your guide." Hailey made a sweeping gesture. "Right this way."

I followed her to the stacks. "Do you know if any of the books include a gwiber?"

"That's what the index is for. I can help you though. I don't mind. Anything to avoid their sticky hands." She inclined her head toward the toddler pit.

"I'm surprised you'd let them in the library with sticky hands. Seems like a bad idea."

"They only touch the board books that can be wiped down during story time. It's an unofficial rule that, thankfully, most people follow." She narrowed her eyes at the gaggle of children. "I'm looking at you, Jeremy Flint." She pulled a handful of books off the shelves. "Start with these."

Hailey stood behind me, watching as I perused the books. I knew she was there to be helpful, but I felt the weight of her stare pressing between my shoulder blades. It was deeply unsettling.

I plucked the top book from the pile and flipped to the back. I stopped when my finger landed on 'gwiber' in the index. "Found something." I flipped to the designated page. The information only filled two paragraphs and didn't tell me anything I didn't already know.

"Thanks for your help, Hailey. I appreciate it."

"No problem. I love helping our patrons and, bonus, now I know what a gwiber is." She began sliding the books back onto the shelf. "I found my calling in life early."

I closed the book and handed it to her. "Everyone should be so lucky."

"You haven't found yours?" She sounded vaguely sympathetic.

There was no easy answer to her question. "I know what I'm good at," I said vaguely.

"That's a good start. A lot of people don't even get that far. There's so much self-doubt and self-criticism."

I smiled. "Oh, I do that, too."

Hailey returned the smile. "I think we're all guilty of that on occasion."

I left the library feeling a mixture of relief and dread. The gwiber had already taken lives—what if one of those lives belonged to Ashley? What if my ghostly radar missed her for some reason? No, Camryn also determined that she was alive, both here and not here. Of course that could mean that Ashley was bordering on death. And even if she was alive, the gwiber was still at large, albeit without fangs. I'd tell the pack everything I knew about the monster and hoped that would be enough.

"I've never heard of a gwiber," Nana Pratt said. The ghosts had accosted me the second my foot hit the porch, and I allowed them to accompany me inside.

"They're not common anywhere, even in their home country."

"What kind of snake are we talking about?" Ray asked.

"It's like a giant adder," I said.

"And it's poisonous on top of everything else," he said.

"Venomous. The fangs inject you with a toxin. That's what killed Arthur, the werewolf."

"Does it matter?" Nana Pratt asked. "Not about Arthur, of course that matters. I mean that it's venomous."

"It means I can jump on its back and not worry about absorbing any toxins."

"Why would you want to jump on its back?" Nana and Ray asked in unison.

"I'm just explaining why it's helpful to know."

"Are you sure you're equipped to fight a thing like that?" Ray asked with concern.

"I'm a decent fighter."

Nana Pratt's face softened. "Yes, but *why* are you a decent fighter? It's not like ghosts fight back."

I wore a wry smile. "You'd be surprised."

"Ask the wolf pack for help," Ray insisted. "They'll want to be rid of the monster as much as you. It already killed one of theirs. It's only a matter of time before there are more casualties."

"I'm with Ray on this. I don't like you putting yourself in harm's way."

"I appreciate your concern. You'll be happy to know the wolves and I are helping each other with the gwiber."

"All I see is a hammer and a chainsaw," Ray said. "I owned a shotgun. Maybe it's still available."

"I don't think a gun is the answer." Or a hammer or a chainsaw. "The gwiber lives in water and on land."

"Lorelei is right," Nana said. "If this thing is hiding in water, a gun is useless."

"What bodies of water are in the area that are large enough to hide a gwiber?" I asked. "I know the Falls and the Delaware River."

"And the creek," Ray added. "Depending on how skinny the creature is."

"There's Bridger Pond," Nana Pratt said, "but I think they would've noticed a giant snake on their property by now."

"Bridger," I repeated. "As in Penelope?"

"Yes, the farm has been in the Bridger family for generations," Nana said.

And the current Bridgers were all accounted for. It was unlikely the creature would bypass the closest meal in search of another one.

"The men have been missing from that farm, but that's been as far back as I can remember," Ray chimed in. "I don't think it has anything to do with the gwiber."

"The Bridgers are witches," I announced. You could've heard an ant marching across the floorboards.

Nana Pratt's brow furrowed. "I'm sorry, dear. My hearing doesn't seem to be any better in the afterlife. Did you say the Bridgers are witches?"

"I did, and they are. Kelsey is a witch. Remember the redhead who delivered the ward?"

Ray scratched his translucent head. "I don't understand. Can witches reproduce on their own like those sea creatures I saw in a documentary?"

I laughed. "No. They find a willing man somewhere else and then return to their coven to carry the child to term."

"What if they have a boy?" Nana's fingers crept along her neckline as she contemplated the awful possibilities. "They don't…"

"They only produce girls," I replied.

"Imagine that. Witches right here in Fairhaven." Nana glanced out the window. "A shame to discover all this fascinating information after I'm dead. I would've liked to know more."

"You'll know more now," Ray told her. "Better late than never."

I let them continue their wonderment while I formulated a plan. I was beginning to rethink my decision to track the monster alone, not because I needed reinforcements, but because there was simply too much ground for one person to cover. The information about bodies of water was helpful; it could explain why the wolves were unable to track the creature the last time.

I swiped my phone off the counter and dialed West's number.

"Oh, good. She's doing as she's told," I heard Nana Pratt say to Ray. "More than my Ashley was capable of."

West answered on the third ring, and I gave him the update, including the fact that it could live on land or in water, which made it harder to track.

"The good news is it can be killed by mortal means." No need for Poseidon's trident or Thor's hammer to defeat the beast. Small mercies. Of course, we still needed a plan.

"I'll assemble a team, and we'll meet you near the Falls in an hour, if that suits you," he tacked on carefully.

West was clearly accustomed to giving orders; his compulsion to kowtow to me must've rankled him.

I left the phone on the counter and hurried upstairs to gather my gear. I felt Ray and Nana's eyes on me as I pulled a trunk out from under the bed and unlocked it.

"Is that where you keep your diary?" Nana asked.

"I don't have a diary." I flipped up the lid to reveal a cache of weapons.

"Glory be!" Nana cried. "You're keeping those dangerous things right under your bed?"

"Can you think of a more convenient place if an intruder breaks into my bedroom again?" I kept my focus on the selection of weapons. I needed a dagger for close range and a set of throwing knives for longer range.

"If Chief Garcia catches you with all that, she'll arrest you," Nana said.

"She won't catch me." I collected the chosen weapons and headed out.

I climbed into the truck and sped toward the woods. It would take time to hike to the Falls from where I intended to leave the truck, and I didn't want to be late. Knowing West, he'd have them start without me.

The entire pack seemed to be crawling through the woods

by the time I arrived. They didn't seem thrilled to see me. Anna immediately disappeared behind a cluster of trees. Most kept their distance, except West.

"I've got a team checking the river and another one checking the creek," he said. "Do you have any preferences?"

"I was curious to see the Falls."

He grinned. "You think it's hiding behind them?"

"No, I've heard they're impressive is all."

And they were. The Falls roared as water cascaded down the hill, crashing over rocks on its way.

"If you're finished exploring the sights, maybe you could join a search party," West suggested.

"I work better alone."

"Yeah. I'm sure you do." His gaze flicked to the dagger sheathed to my leg. "We're meeting back here at sundown for a head count. Take care of yourself, Clay."

"I always do."

I spent hours traipsing up hills and through the wilderness. I crossed paths with a few werewolves over the course of the day, as well as a herd of deer, a fox, and a multitude of squirrels. Nary a gwiber in sight. No ghosts either, which put my mind at ease. I didn't need another Arthur situation today, and neither did the pack.

The sun had set by the time I returned to the appointed site. I tried not to let my frustration show. Aside from flattened bushes and a short trail of goop, we were no closer to finding the gwiber.

"We'll try again tomorrow," I said, in an effort to sound optimistic.

"Tomorrow night's no good for us," West said.

Instinctively, I glanced skyward. "Full moon?"

"Even better. Strawberry Supermoon."

"What does that mean for your pack? You'll howl louder?"

He chuckled. "It means you might want to avoid the woods. We'll be leaving tufts of fur all over the forest floor."

"Then you'd better hope we catch the gwiber before you let your pack loose, or it could be a bloodbath."

West's expression soured. "That won't happen on my watch."

"Why not? Arthur died on your watch." The moment the words left my mouth, I knew I shouldn't have said them. The werewolf turned cold, and a wall dropped down between us.

"Arthur got separated from us. And if you recall, we were out there because you asked them to be." His voice grew dangerously close to thundering. So much for not pissing off the alpha of the werewolf pack. I knew it was only a matter of time.

"I didn't mean to blame you."

My response had no effect; his face remained stony. "You're lucky Arthur died, because if I hadn't lost one of my own, I'd order the pack to stay out of this from now on. Here, you'll want this back." West withdrew Ashley's bracelet and slapped it into my hand. He shifted right in front of me, planting a powerful roar in my face for good measure before sprinting away.

"Making friends everywhere you go, I see."

I turned to see Kane with his arms folded, leaning casually against a pine tree. In a black collared shirt, black trousers, and shiny black loafers, he looked far too dapper for summer heat in the middle of a forest.

"Careful. Pine needles are sharp," I said. "You wouldn't want them to poke holes in your expensive shirt, although they might give your body some much needed air-conditioning."

He pushed away from the tree and dusted off his sleeve. "Concerned for my body, are you?"

Oomph. I walked right into that one.

"What happened between you and the big dog?"

"None of your business. What are you doing here?"

"I happened to be passing through and heard a commotion."

"Little Red Riding Hood on her way to visit a sick grandmother, is that it?" I didn't believe a word.

"Fine. Everyone at the club was talking about the dead werewolf and today's search party. I decided to confirm the rumors."

"In other words, you're nosy."

"This is my backyard, Miss Clay. It would be unwise to ignore it." He slid his hands into his trouser pockets. I got the sense it was a practiced move; one he'd perfected over the years in an attempt to appear suave and casual. "I would never have guessed a gwiber was the culprit, and it takes a lot to surprise me."

I looked at him closely. "You're a demon. Can't you locate one of your distant cousins through a psychic link?"

Kane cracked a smile. "I have no connection to the gwiber whatsoever."

"Too bad. You might've actually been useful."

His eyes danced with mischief. "Demons are useful in other ways, I assure you."

"No need for assurances." Been there. Got the bite marks to prove it.

"I do think your theory is correct," Kane said.

"Which one?"

"I believe the gwiber is the reason for the girl's disappearance."

"If she's hiding, why can't we find her?" It seemed unlikely that Ashley was clever enough to outwit me, the monster, and an entire wolf pack.

"Perhaps she inadvertently passed through a gateway in her attempt to elude the creature."

I remembered Gwen's reference to the crossroads. Fear coiled in the pit of my stomach. "Is that possible?"

"If the gwiber can come here, why not the other way around?"

My pulse raced. "Are you aware of previous occurrences?" No one had mentioned that Fairhaven had a history of missing persons; it seemed to me that would've been relevant to Ashley's case.

"I can't claim to keep up with human investigations. You'd have to ask your new friend, the police chief."

I wasn't in a hurry to speak to Chief Garcia again. Then again, I owed her an update on Ashley. It might be a good time to show her that I'm a helpful, law-abiding citizen.

Before she learned otherwise.

CHAPTER 16

The next morning Chief Garcia invited me to meet her at Five Beans, the coffee shop on Main Street, to deliver my update in person. My update was to say I had no new information; I couldn't exactly tell her about the gwiber. I did, however, want to dig into any local history of missing persons. If there was one, *The Complete History of Fairhaven* neglected to mention it.

"I hear you're becoming a regular at Hewitt's," the chief said. We stood at the end of the line inside the coffee shop. "I bet Clark appreciates the business."

"The downside of buying a fixer upper is definitely an upside for Clark."

She gestured to the counter. "Their pastries are homemade. I recommend the cinnamon bun. It's a thousand calories, but you'll work it off in one afternoon with all that manual labor you've been doing."

The sight and smell of the sticky cinnamon bun was too tempting to resist. "Worth it."

"Do you invite all residents for coffee?" I asked, once we were seated with our purchases.

"Only the mysterious ones from another country."

"I only lived abroad temporarily."

"London, right? How was it?"

"Damp."

She smiled. "I've never been to London. I've never been anywhere outside the US."

"No interest?"

"No time. A day of travel on either end doesn't leave much time to enjoy the days in-between, plus the time change." Shrugging, she took a generous bite of her cinnamon bun.

"Fairhaven seems like a nice place to pass the time at least."

She laughed. "Is that how you describe your life—passing the time?"

"Only when I'm making awkward small talk."

"Fair enough."

As I bit into the sweet pastry, cinnamon and sugar flooded my taste buds. I felt like I could taste each and every delicious calorie. I almost didn't want to swallow. "You weren't kidding. This is phenomenal."

"And Rita won't share the recipe," Chief Garcia said, loudly enough for the owner to hear. "Even with the police chief."

"My grandmother would roll over in her grave," Rita shot back.

Smiling, the chief tipped back her coffee cup and drank. I silently wondered whether Rita's grandmother was magical; I doubted a garden-variety human could conjure a recipe this exquisite.

"Would you really make this yourself if you had the recipe?" I asked. "I think food tastes better when someone else makes it."

"You sound like my ex-girlfriend. That was her excuse for never cooking dinner."

"When you live alone, it's either cook or get takeout."

"Your house is big enough for a live-in chef. You might want to consider it."

"My bank account won't let me."

"Mine barely lets me enjoy the bounty in front of me, such is life in the public sector," the chief countered. "So, what's your update? Since there's been no sign of Ashley, I'm guessing she's still missing."

"Afraid so. She hasn't contacted Steven, and I've spoken to people in town, but no leads have panned out so far." I kept my promise to Lyra and didn't mention her unfortunate encounter with an animal. In light of recent developments, it was possible Lyra had, in fact, been attacked by an actual bear and Theo was just a jerk who ghosted her. Her marks hadn't been made by a gwiber, and she would've been able to identify a giant snake.

Chief Garcia stared into her coffee cup as though in a trance. "I was worried you were going to say that," she finally said. Her voice dropped to a murmur. "We found a body."

My heart skipped a beat. "Were you able to identify them?"

"Sorry, it wasn't Ashley. I should've made that clear." Her gaze darted left to right to make sure no one was eavesdropping. "Her name was Anya Swanson."

Anya.

Why did I know that name?

Why is it that women named Anya are always whores?

Shit. Otto's ex. "What happened?"

"Looks like another animal attack, but at least we have a body this time. It was covered in tiny marks, like she'd been stabbed by a thousand tiny knives. The coroner is going to have his hands full trying to identify the animal that did that to her."

My stomach turned. "Where did you find her?"

"Wild Acres. A hiker called it in right near the Knob." She

paused. "He found her head first. Her body was about twenty feet away."

"Any idea when she was killed?"

"Not exactly, but her body was still warm when she was found."

"When was that?"

"Around sunrise this morning."

I nearly spat out my coffee. The gwiber had been defanged. There was no way Anya's body would've been warm and covered in fang wounds if she'd been killed by the gwiber.

"Did she lose a lot of blood?" I asked.

The chief wore a rueful smile. "That tends to happen when someone's been decapitated."

A severed head and a body full of tiny holes. Anya Swanson had been treated like a human pinata.

"Now I really wish I'd made progress finding Ashley."

"You and me both." She took a troubled sip of her coffee.

"I have a more general question," I began. "Does Fairhaven have a history of missing people?"

"Not to my knowledge."

"You're the police chief. Who else would know if not you?"

"I've only been chief for a couple years. You're talking about the history of a very old town."

I smiled. "Old by American standards."

"What makes you ask about missing people?" the chief asked.

"Just a library book I was reading," I lied.

"It's nice to know you're brushing up on local history."

"I know I'm not an official investigator, but would you tell me what the coroner says about the cause of death?"

Her eyebrows drew together. "Normally, I'd say no, but maybe by some stroke of luck, he'll find evidence that will lead us to Ashley." Despite her words, the chief didn't look hopeful.

"Thank you. And do me a favor. Don't tell Steven about Anya Swanson." I didn't want him to worry any more than he already was.

"No problem. I plan to keep this as quiet as I can until I have more information. I'm only telling you because…" She leaned back and assessed me. "To be honest, I didn't intend to tell you. In hindsight, I probably shouldn't have, but this whole thing is making me think twice about Ashley, and you've been doing the legwork there."

"You still don't trust me."

"Let's recap. You're a newcomer in town. You keep to yourself. You don't show up at bingo night or any of the local events to meet people. You don't seem eager to make friends. A girl goes missing, and you happen to be the one searching for her, even though you have no connection to her." She pinned me with a hard look. "Can you blame me?"

"No. I wouldn't trust me either in your position."

Although her expression didn't soften, I noticed her grip loosen on her coffee cup. "Thanks for meeting me in person."

"You introduced me to the cinnamon roll. I'll be forever grateful."

The chief rose to her feet. "I'll let you finish yours in peace. We'll talk soon."

Sadly, there would be no peace, despite the heavenly pastry. Anya's death made sure of that. At least a portion of the wounds would be the handiwork of vampires, given her reputation as a fang banger. Even the missing head could be the result of an overeager vampire, but that was assuming a vampire killed her. Without examining her, I couldn't identify whether the most recent marks were also vampiric in nature. Ignorant humans wouldn't recognize the difference between an animal attack and vampire bites, although I couldn't think of a single animal in the natural world that would've left Anya in such a horrific state. And if it wasn't the gwiber—

Then there was another monster in town.

Upon leaving Five Beans, I did the thing I swore to myself I wouldn't do.

He picked up on the first ring. "Kane Sullivan."

"Are you busy right now, Mr. Sullivan?"

"For you, Miss Clay? Never."

I rolled my eyes, not that he could see me. Then again, he was a mysterious demon. Maybe he could. "Meet me at the Knob in twenty minutes."

"Why not ask your furry friend?"

Boy, those two *really* didn't like each other. "What makes you think I didn't?"

"Because you'd be a fool to call me as well, and I've already determined that you're no fool."

I hesitated. "You saw how West and I left things. I don't think he'll want to hear from me."

"And why do you need my help? I thought you were an independent woman. The Greta Garbo of supernaturals."

"A Greta Garbo reference? Careful, Mr. Sullivan. Your age is showing."

"Or perhaps only my taste in films."

"A woman was found dead early this morning near the Knob. I want to search the area before it's crawling with cops."

"What makes you think it isn't already?"

"Because Chief Garcia is keeping it quiet for now, and she's currently heading back to her office with a stomach full of cinnamon roll." If I were strictly human, I'd be resting my head on the desk for an hour in order to digest all those carbs.

"Very well then. I'll be there."

True to his word, the demon arrived at the Knob a couple

minutes after me. He was dressed in more casual attire this morning. In lieu of his trademark starched shirt and trousers, he wore black jeans and a black T-shirt that stretched across his broad shoulders. With that body, he could've worn a hot dog costume and still looked undeniably sexy. Life wasn't fair, as Anya Swanson would agree.

A rectangle of yellow tape was the obvious sign of this morning's discovery. Upon closer inspection, there was still blood on the ground, as well as on nearby fallen branches. The chief wouldn't be able to keep this quiet for very long. It was summer, and people hiked to the Knob every day.

Kane observed the scene with a slight curl of his upper lip that I translated to distaste. "It's a surprisingly large area. How big was this woman?"

"Her head was found at one end and her body was found at another."

He circled the tape, eyeing the blood spatter as he walked. "And what makes you think I'll make a worthy detective? I have no special tracking abilities."

"No, but if you can read a crime scene as well as you can read a room, I'll consider you an asset."

His eyes sparked with delight. "A compliment, Miss Clay? I shall mark this day on my calendar." He crouched to examine one of the bloody branches inside the protected area. "Quite a lot of blood. Are we certain it's hers?"

"No, but the condition of her body suggests it is."

"And you don't think the gwiber is responsible?"

"Based on the chief's description, her body was covered in puncture wounds, but the gwiber's fangs were removed by the time this occurred. I don't see how."

He resumed an upright position. "Perhaps the fangs regenerate like the arm of a starfish."

"Not to my knowledge, and even if they did, I doubt it would've happened so quickly."

He scanned the area outside the yellow tape. "What was she doing out here alone?"

"Maybe she wasn't alone. Or maybe her body was left here to be found." A spot like the Knob guaranteed a body would be discovered.

He cut a sidelong glance at me. "You think this woman was killed by something other than a monster?"

"I honestly don't know. I'm keeping my options open."

His mouth quirked. "Sounds like my dating habits."

We searched the surrounding area without success. No ghost. No new evidence. No signs of a struggle. Nothing.

"Given the victim's history and the recent rumors about trafficking, it could be vampires."

Kane looked at me with surprise. "Do you really think that's likely?"

"She was known to enjoy their company a little too much," I said. "She was riddled with holes and decapitated."

"But was she drained dry? And why was her body left here, where it would surely be found? I have a hard time believing the vampires would demonstrate such a blatant disregard for the delicate balance amongst supernaturals in Fairhaven."

A plausible rebuttal. "Another monster then."

He regarded the crime scene again. "Perhaps." He removed a white cloth from his pocket and wiped his hands, stuffing it back into his pocket when he finished. "Come with me, Miss Clay. I'd like to show you something."

"Where?"

He must've detected a note of suspicion in my voice because he asked, "Would you feel better if I left a trail of breadcrumbs? Perhaps a spool of thread?"

"They won't do me much good if I'm dead."

He clucked his tongue. "Come now, Miss Clay. We both know it wouldn't be that easy to kill you."

It was only a guess, I knew, but he guessed right.

"What do you want to show me?" I asked.

His mouth turned up at the corners. "The only way to know is to come with me. Seriously, Miss Clay, you trusted me enough to search the area with you."

"That's because I wanted to watch you."

His brow lifted. "Oh, I see. You wanted to see whether I displayed any prior knowledge of the crime scene."

"I wanted to rule you out."

"And have you?"

"I have."

"Good." He beckoned me forward. "I hope those shoes are comfortable. It's best to travel there on foot."

We walked in relative silence until we reached a section of the woods about twenty feet north of the Falls. I couldn't tell whether he was waiting for me to initiate conversation. If so, I sorely disappointed him.

Kane stood in front of two mighty oak trees and opened his arms wide. "Behold, the crossroads."

I stared at the trees, underwhelmed. "This is it?"

He twisted to regard me. "Yes. I think this is where the monster came from."

I surveyed the area. "What makes you think that? I don't see any evidence." No destruction. No fallen trees.

Kane sighed wearily. "You're very difficult to impress, Miss Clay. Do you think I offer personal tours to just anybody?"

No, I didn't. Kane Sullivan clearly did whatever he liked, whenever he liked, with whomever he liked. Nice gig if you can get it.

I approached the gateway. No doubt it was the same one Matilda and Gwen had passed through to get here. The same one Kane had referenced yesterday when he basically said a door works both ways.

"Is this the only gateway in the area?"

He dragged a hand through his hair. "Do you really want to know?"

"I think it's important."

"Yes. This is the only one in Fairhaven, but the crossroads here are special."

"Let me guess. Because you live here?"

He pressed a hand to his chest in a mocking gesture. "You flatter me, Miss Clay. No, because the crossroads here are unlike any other, to my knowledge. They seem to be a place where multiple gateways converge."

I started to choke. "Are you serious?"

"Occasionally."

I stared at the seemingly innocuous oak trees, absorbing the news. I'd never heard of such a thing. It had to be an anomaly.

"How many?" I asked.

"Infinite, as far as I can tell. It serves as an intersection of all the realms."

"All," I repeated, somewhat dazed.

"I assume. It's a rather difficult thing to verify, as you can imagine."

I shook my head. "This can't be right. A crossroads is where two realms meet." I held up two fingers.

"Typically, yes. Fairhaven seems to be unique in that respect."

I could feel my blood pressure rising. "And there's no liminal deity here?"

He raised an eyebrow.

"A god or goddess of crossroads. They watch over thresholds, gates, doorways. Anywhere there's a boundary to cross."

He gave me a blank look.

"Enodia? Hecate? Janus? Any of those names ring a bell?"

"You seem to know a lot about them."

I ignored his remark. "You would think a crossroads this

powerful would require a liminal deity to look after it."

"Perhaps you haven't noticed, but deities seem to be in short supply these days."

I was well aware, more than he knew. "There was no mention of this in the books I read from the library."

"Does that surprise you?"

Not really. Books written by humans were woefully inaccurate with the information they did contain, never mind all the information that was missing.

I shook my head. "I seriously can't believe there's no one guarding this."

"For what purpose?"

"To kill anything that comes through."

"Seems a rather harsh penalty for immigrants," he said.

Fair point. "Why didn't you tell me about this sooner? You acted like it was insignificant." But it wasn't. This explained Fairhaven as a supernatural magnet. The waterfall was likely acting as a conductor, absorbing the supernatural energy generated by multiple gates and spreading it through the surrounding area that included the Wild Acres and Fairhaven.

"I wasn't sure whether I could trust you," Kane said.

I barked a laugh. "Trust me? I'm the one trying to save the life of an innocent girl."

He gave me an appreciative look. "For a woman trying to live in isolation, you seem to care a lot about the fate of some random human you've never met."

"I don't have to meet her to know she doesn't deserve to die a horrible death."

"Then you believe that people are inherently good."

"I didn't say that." In truth, it was their nightmares that persuaded me they deserved better. The palpable fear. The merciless way they torment themselves. Humans were harder on themselves than any god could ever be. "Tell me more about the crossroads."

"What do you want to know?"

I waved a hand at the blank space. "Is this how you got here? You walked through the gateway from whichever circle of hell you came from."

"More or less."

Fabulous. Leave it to me to make hell my neighbor, because a cemetery wasn't enough.

"The crossroads are marked by these symbols. Once you know where they are, they're easy to find." He tapped the trunk of the oak tree on the left.

I peered at the design and immediately recognized the Nordic symbol for Yggdrasil, the tree of life. To the human eye, the design simply looked like the artistic carving of a tree on another tree. To those in the know, however, Yggdrasil represented much more—a tree connected to the realms of the universe. According to Norse legends, there were nine realms. It seemed that the Norse had vastly underestimated.

"How often do you travel home?" I asked.

"This is my home now," he replied in a clipped tone.

"And why is that? What's so great about Fairhaven that you'd give up your homeland?"

"I like the seasons. There's only one in hell. It becomes draining after too long."

"Is this like *Death Takes a Holiday*? Are you summering in the mortal world the way robber barons summered in Newport?"

Kane looked down his nose at me. "You have a strange mind, Lorelei Clay."

Too much time with ghosts had that effect on a person. "Why are you involved with the Assassins Guild?"

Closing his eyes, he sighed. "This again?"

"It seems like a strange activity. Why not coach the soccer team or run the PTA?"

"Do I strike you as someone who would do either one of those things?"

"Not in that outfit, maybe, but in the right clothes…"

He looked down at his outfit. "What's wrong with my attire? It's suitably casual."

"It's distracting," I blurted. "I mean, for the humans. All that black."

Kane gave a rueful shake of his head. "I'm starting to understand why you prefer to keep to yourself."

"Right back at you."

"I don't keep to myself. In fact, I'm very social. Ask anyone at my club."

"But it's an act," I shot back. "Tell the truth. I don't care how many hot vampires you surround yourself with. You would much rather be alone."

He flinched. "There's nothing wrong with enjoying attractive company. You should try it sometime."

"I have all the company I need," I said, thinking of Nana Pratt and Ray. My house was already more crowded than I intended it to be. I'd left London to live in solitude, and I'd already managed to pick up two strays. I should've forced them to cross over with the rest of the spirits. Then I'd be in my living room right now with my headphones on, a paint roller in one hand, and a beer in the other.

"I can post guards here to see whether any monsters pass in or out," Kane offered. "I should've done it before now. I didn't realize how dire the situation would become. The supernatural factions have fared well over the years. I thought there was no need to fix what isn't broken, as the saying goes."

I thought of poor Arthur. "I'm not sure the Arrowhead pack would agree." An uneasy thought occurred to me. "You mentioned yesterday that Ashley might've inadvertently passed through here to escape the gwiber. What if you're right? What if she wandered into a realm like yours?"

His expression turned grim. "Then I'm afraid she won't be coming back."

CHAPTER 17

Anya Swanson was easy in more ways than one. She was a known fang banger among supernaturals in town. If someone wanted to pin the animal attacks and the missing girl on vampires, Anya's death was an obvious choice. But if that were true, then it meant we were dealing with more than a gwiber. Was someone controlling the monster and, if so, for what purpose? Maybe the gwiber returned to its master without fangs, and Anya was a message to the rest of us to back off. Not a very clear message. And I still had no idea how to find Ashley.

"You're very expressive when you're deep in thought," Kane said. He'd escorted me to my truck for no apparent reason, and I'd been too preoccupied to shake him off.

"I'm going to Ashley's house." There was one more trick I hadn't tried, mainly because it required me to use my power, the kind of power that could draw unwanted attention if it were noticed.

"How may I be of service?" When I shot him a sharp look, he shrugged. "What? I told you missing young women are bad for business. I'd like to assist you however I can."

"What would you do?" I opened the door of the truck and climbed behind the wheel.

He contemplated the question. "Search the room for signs of the occult. Perhaps she summoned a demon and was taken. Have you considered that?"

"Maybe I would have if you'd been up front about the crossroads sooner. Get in."

On the drive to Ashley's, I called Otto to break the news about Anya because it seemed like the right thing to do. He took it well; like most vampires, he had experience with loss.

"It wasn't vampires," he said. "The severed head was a mistake. We would never do that. It wastes too much blood."

"Not even a vampire suffering from bloodlust?"

"Then she would've been drained dry, and it sounds like she wasn't."

I snuck a quick peek at Kane, who'd said the same.

"Knowing Anya's proclivities for sex and violence, she would've enjoyed an overly enthusiastic vampire, as you put it." Otto paused. "I thought I would feel happy when she was finally hoisted by her own petard."

"But you don't?"

"No, I feel only pity for her. Is there any chance you could speak to her spirit and find out what happened to her?"

"She wasn't there. I assume she crossed over before I got there." Not all spirits wanted or needed my help.

"Then her soul is at rest."

"I believe it is."

"That is some comfort. Thank you." He hung up.

Kane raised his eyebrows. "A show of kindness for Otto Visconti? My, you really are full of surprises."

I gripped the steering wheel. "It wasn't kindness. It was... I just thought he should know."

I could feel Kane's smirk the remainder of the drive to the house. I parked in the driveway of the modest two-story house and was relieved to see Steven's car there. I wondered how much it was costing him to take time off work during this crisis. He was already in over his head with his parents' mortgage, according to the chief.

I rang the doorbell and glanced at Kane. "Minimal speaking. I don't want to frighten Steven."

The door split open, revealing a sleepy Steven with a stubbled jawline. He wore a wrinkled T-shirt and running shorts. "Hey," he said groggily.

"I'm sorry we woke you."

He rubbed his eyes. "You didn't. I keep trying to sleep, but my mind won't turn off."

I knew how that felt. "This is Kane Sullivan. He's helping me."

"Any news?" Steven's voice cracked with hope.

"No, but there's something I haven't tried yet." There was no way I was telling him about Anya, not when he looked like he was on the cusp of a breakdown.

"What is it?"

"I can't tell you."

Steven gave me a searching look. "Can't or won't?"

"Won't," I said firmly. I came to Fairhaven to start fresh. I wasn't about to reveal my secret now, and to a human. Someone like Steven, with only minimal knowledge of the supernatural world, would see me as a threat instead of an ally. The fact that I could communicate with ghosts was likely outside of his comfort zone, but he was willing to grin and bear it for Ashley's sake. Any more information would tip the scales of tolerance.

Steven tugged at his unkempt hair, appearing to arrive at a decision. "Okay. What do you need from me?"

"Ashley's bedroom."

He frowned. "You want to try to contact her spirit again?"

"Sort of," I said. "It isn't the way I normally operate, so it might not work, but it's worth a try."

Steven offered a curt nod. "I trust you. Her bedroom's upstairs. First door on the left."

"Thanks. You should wait here." I cut across the small foyer to the bottom of the staircase.

I darted up the steps, conscious of Kane's direct view of my backside. I turned quickly at the top of the staircase and spilled straight into Ashley's bedroom.

The room seemed to be in a state of arrested development. The pink walls were the shade of a ballerina slipper. Butterfly sun catchers dangled from the ceiling. It was as though the room hadn't been altered in years—and maybe it hadn't. My own childhood bedroom had become a time capsule after my grandmother died. It didn't occur to Pops to update anything, nor did it occur to me to ask. I lacked the self-awareness to know I wanted anything at all, other than to fit in with the other children. My focus had been entirely external—be like everyone else. Belong. My primary goal had been to stay in whatever school I was in at the time. I failed far more often than I succeeded.

"Someone is a fan of pink," Kane commented as he inspected the contents of the room.

"What would a demon notice that I wouldn't?" I asked.

He picked up a handheld mirror and took a moment to admire his refection. "I'll let you know when I find it."

The bed was unmade and littered with pillows. "She likes to feel cozy," I surmised.

"Who doesn't?" Kane moved from the mirror to a jewelry box on the dresser. "Nothing of interest in here. Not even a single crystal."

I glanced up. "Did you expect to find evidence of magic?"

He closed the lid of the jewelry box. "Not her own. I wondered whether someone had been grooming her for another purpose. Young women are more susceptible…"

I glared at him. "You'd better stop right there. I don't want Steven to have to break up a fight between us."

Kane grunted. "As though that were even possible."

"Because he's human?"

"No, because it wouldn't be much of a fight." He spared a casual glance over his shoulder at me. "You'd be dead before he reached the first step."

"I thought you said I had power."

He turned back to the dresser and picked up a squat candle. "And like Josie said, you resist using it, which means you'd be out of practice with—whatever it is you do." He sniffed the candle and grimaced. "Bubblegum, I think. Vile." He set the candle on the dresser. "Well, Ashley Pratt seems like a quite ordinary girl."

"You sound disappointed."

"I like a little spice in my humans."

I arched an eyebrow. "*Your* humans?"

"I meant it in an affectionate way rather than proprietary."

Steven poked his head in the doorway. "See anything helpful?"

I gave Kane a pointed look. "Not at the moment." I motioned to the Lake Placid movie poster. "Your sister doesn't strike me as a horror fan."

Steven broke into a smile. "I put it there a few years ago as a joke. When she was nine, she begged our parents to watch the movie and ended up regretting it. We even had to leave the crocodile enclosure at the zoo that summer." His smile faded. "I'm a real dick."

"No, you're a big brother," I said.

"Can't I be both?" His cheeks reddened. "What if that's the last thing she remembers about me?"

"She was nine," I said. "I'm sure it's been long forgotten." And the fact that she'd left the poster intact all these years was a sign of her affection for her brother.

"I thought you were going to wait for us downstairs." Kane steered Steven out of the bedroom.

"I wanted to check if you need anything. I don't have much at the moment. I can offer you water or a protein bar."

"We're good, thanks." I sat on the edge of Ashley's bed and examined the items on the bedside table. There was a blank journal, presumably purchased for the pretty floral cover, as well as a stuffed grey cat. My gaze lingered on the cat. This wasn't my usual method, so I wasn't sure which personal item might allow me to access Ashley's nightmares.

"Give me a shout if you…" Kane closed the door before Steven could finish his statement.

I reached across the bed and hefted the sparkly pink pillow in the shape of the letter 'A.' "I'm going to use this." I wiggled my fingers. "Move along now. There's no need to stay in the room. It's distracting."

"What? No spooning? How disappointing. I even wore my softest shirt."

I pointed to the door. "Out."

The demon left but not before flashing one last mischievous smile. I still didn't understand his willingness to help. He categorized a lot of things as 'bad for business' that seemed to have no connection to the Devil's Playground. Ashley had disappeared from Monk's in a different section of town, and nobody was pointing the finger at demons.

Although maybe they should be. As I set the decorative pillow on my lap, I pondered whether Kane's ulterior motive could be to mask his own involvement. What better way to cover his tracks than to 'assist' me in my investigation? Although I'd watched him at Anya's crime scene and everything had seemed genuinely new to him, that didn't mean he was innocent in connection to Ashley. Anya's death could be unrelated.

Or maybe he simply wanted to know more about my hidden powers and thought that staying close to me would yield the answers. That I understood. I'd been thinking of returning to the club for the same purpose.

I closed my eyes and concentrated on the fluffy pillow. I pictured Ashley hugging the pillow to her chest, the soft material absorbing her tears. She'd endured a fair amount of heartbreak in her short years. I felt like I understood her; maybe that was the real reason I'd agreed to help Steven. The computer had been an excuse to justify my involvement to myself.

Eventually, the pillow dissipated, and I was touching—nothing. A void.

I threw the pillow across the room in frustration.

I fell back against the regular pillow and tried to get comfortable. If I could tap into the right nightmare, I might find Ashley. I closed my eyes, focusing on the emotions associated with Ashley's disappearance. Steven's sense of responsibility following the death of their parents. Nana Pratt's concern.

There was no easy way to prepare for entry into the land of nightmares. I'd be used to them by now if I were more willing to use my abilities.

My mind flashed through a series of unsettling images. A few were more humorous than scary, like one that featured a talking hat, although it was unlikely funny to the person experiencing the dream. My heart rate increased as the horrors intensified. I stopped the mental page from turning when my mind's eye snagged on a familiar place.

Monk's.

Someone had experienced a nightmare about the dive bar. To be fair, some dive bars were a living nightmare, but Monk's wasn't one of them.

The counter and stools were splashed with blood. Patrons were sprawled across the floor. A young woman rose from the heap of bodies. Despite the cuts and bruises, I recognized her face.

Ashley Pratt.

Her T-shirt and shorts were torn. Thorny vines broke

through the wooden floor on either side of her; they twisted around her body like serpents, holding her in place. Worms pushed through her eye sockets.

She opened her mouth and screamed.

I bolted upright in response to the earsplitting sound. I heard the sound of ragged breathing and realized it was my own. Fading beams of sunlight streamed into my bedroom.

My bedroom? How did I get here?

I untangled the damp and twisted sheets that were wrapped around my legs.

"Welcome back, sunshine," a smooth voice said.

I leapt from the bed. Kane sat in the oversized chair in the corner of my bedroom.

"What in the hell are you doing here?" I demanded.

He held up a book—my well-worn copy of *Pride & Prejudice*. "Reading, until I was rudely interrupted by your scream. I'm desperate to know what happens to Lydia."

I steadied my breathing. "What are you doing in my room?" I ground out.

"I delivered you safely home after you collapsed. You've been out for hours." He set the book aside and stood. "What were you dreaming about? It was either horrific or very pornographic." He tilted his head. "Perhaps both."

Ray materialized in the doorway. "He carried you inside. I was worried you were dead, so I came in to check on you. Once I saw your chest rising and falling, I felt better."

"He was a perfect gentleman," Nana Pratt added, appearing beside Ray. "He didn't even undress you. Just placed you in your bed and watched over you, and not like one of those perverts."

I looked down at my clothes. Nana was right, this was my outfit from earlier.

I shifted my focus to Kane. "I collapsed in Ashley's room?"

"Whatever you attempted to do must have overloaded

your system. I heard a thumping noise and returned to the bedroom. I thought you were having a seizure. Usually when I pin a woman down to a bed, it's because she requested it." His mouth quirked. "One might even say she begged."

I didn't know what to say. Nothing like that had ever happened to me before. The nightmares themselves didn't disturb me; nightmares coursed through my veins as naturally as blood. What bothered me was that I lost control to the point of losing consciousness. I blamed Steven and my visit to Ashley's bedroom; the personal connection had thrown me off my game. Pops would disagree. He believed there was nothing more personal than the ability to invade and control someone's nightmares. Their nightmares revealed their deepest fears and allowed me to wield them as weapons. Although I knew he didn't mean to, my grandfather had shamed me for my ability, as though I'd volunteered for it. I never forgot the way it made me feel.

"Thank you for bringing me home," I said.

"What do you remember?" Kane asked.

"Not that much." I struggled to pull the pieces of the nightmare into place. I'd already been to the bar where Ashley had last been seen. I wasn't sure what the nightmare revealed.

His gaze swept the room. "I find the lack of pink walls reassuring, although you may want to consider a pop of color here and there. One's home should never feel like a prison."

"I'll call you the next time I need design tips." I nudged him toward the doorway.

"The keys to your truck are on the counter. And you might want to ring your friend, Steven. He was distraught when I carried you from the house."

"Did anybody else see you?"

"Not to worry, I was discreet. One of my best qualities, you'll find."

"It's almost as though you have practice in stealing women away under everyone's noses."

"Are you accusing me of something, Miss Clay? If so, I can assure you that you have the wrong supernatural being. I have many red marks in my ledger, but Ashley Pratt isn't one of them." His whisky-colored eyes focused on me. "I have a question for you. Why did you refuse to shake my hand when we first met?"

"I didn't refuse. I just … didn't."

"Is it because I'm a demon? Because I'll tell you right now, that sort of prejudice is not welcome in Fairhaven." The demon paused. "At least, not in the Devil's Playground." He tapped the doorjamb. "Lovely house, by the way. Heaps of potential." He gave the room an admiring glance before leaving it.

Nana Pratt and Ray exchanged looks.

"He's very polite," Nana said diplomatically.

"Why did the house let him in?" Ray asked. "I thought he needed an invitation."

"He isn't a vampire." I kept my voice down in case Kane had lingered downstairs.

"What is he then?" Ray asked, mimicking my whisper, not that Kane could hear him anyway.

"Some sort of demon."

Gasping, Nana clutched her imaginary pearls. "You don't say."

"I hate to break it to you, but he's not the only one in Fairhaven either."

Nana Pratt drifted across the room to the window and peered outside. "You think you know everything about a place…" She turned to face me. "I was born and raised in this town. Never left. I don't know why, but I…" She promptly burst into tears.

Ray moved to comfort her.

"What is it?" I asked.

Ray looked at me. "You really can't see it?"

I waved a hand at Nana Pratt. "I can see she's upset about the supernaturals."

"It isn't that simple," Ray replied. "Imagine Fairhaven is a person, someone you've known and loved your whole life, like a parent. Then you die and you discover they had all these secrets they'd kept from you."

"Like a secret family," Nana said between sniffles.

"Or an evil twin," Ray added.

"It makes you question your entire reality," Nana said. "Was Fairhaven the wonderful place I thought it was, or was I an utter fool to love it as much as I did?"

"Does knowing about supernaturals now change anything about your experience here?" I asked. "Does knowing about vampires or werewolves make your childhood any less magical? Does it make you love the people you knew any less?"

"What if one of them was a vampire and I didn't know it?" Nana Pratt asked.

"It's unlikely," I said. "They tend to keep to their own kind here, I've noticed, but even if you found that your favorite hair stylist was actually a werewolf, what difference would it make? She never hurt you. She didn't howl in your ear while she cut your hair."

Nana pressed her palm flat against her ear, as though imagining the scenario.

"Accept the life you lived at face value," I told her. "From what I've gathered, it was a good one."

Nana's head bobbed. "It was. No complaints, except for losing my own child too soon. If only for Steven and Ashley's sake, I wish the universe had been kinder to our family."

"I appreciate you both coming to check on me. Now I'd appreciate it if you'd give me a little privacy." I'd caught a whiff of my body odor and was glad that ghosts didn't retain their sense of smell. I hadn't intended to take a shower, but it seemed my plans would have to change unless I wanted the entire town to get acquainted with my signature scent of death and sweat.

"Sorry for breaking the rules," Ray said. "Again." The duo wisely made themselves scarce.

The water ran lukewarm, refusing to increase to a hotter temperature. One more household problem to solve. I showered anyway, thinking about the nightmare in more detail as I washed the sweat from my hair. One thing I felt confident about was that Ashley was still alive. It had been my working assumption from the start, but now I was certain. Dead people don't have nightmares; I knew this for a fact. Of course, the nightmare *could* belong to someone else; it wasn't necessarily Ashley's, but the evidence weighed heavily in her favor.

As I towel-dried my hair, I glanced at the clock on my phone. It was a reasonable time to drive to Monk's, although I wasn't sure what I expected to find there this time around. I didn't recognize any of the bodies in the nightmare; they seemed more like faceless silhouettes apart from their crimson wounds.

"You're going out after your fainting spell?" Nana Pratt exclaimed in wonder as I passed her on the bridge.

"It wasn't a fainting spell. I'm not a Southern belle. I have a lead on Ashley, and I want to follow it up."

"Then by all means, carry on." Nana Pratt motioned with her hands for me to keep going. "Is that nice demon gentleman going with you?"

"No. I'm better off handling this on my own."

Loud music blasted from the open windows of Monk's. It was a warm night with a clear sky and low humidity, and locals were taking advantage of the beautiful weather by drinking at the outdoor tables. One drunken group was playing cornhole, which seemed to consist of throwing the beanbags at each other's heads.

I ducked inside and scanned the room. I recalled the details of my nightmare and tried to match any bodies or objects to them. No luck.

I spotted Lyra's familiar face in the crowd. She seemed to have recovered from her animal encounter. Her hair was styled in neat curls, and she wore a white tank top with material so thin, you could see the leopard print of her bra. She was pounding shots with two guys.

Lyra's gaze met mine. As I lifted my hand in greeting, she fled. I was so taken aback by her reaction that she made it outside before I caught up with her.

"Where are you off to in such a hurry?" I grabbed her by the elbow and steered her around the corner, out of sight of the parking lot. "Is your car in danger of turning into a pumpkin?"

She tried to pull away. "Let go of me. What do you think you're doing?"

"I think you and I need to have a conversation."

Lyra spat at my shoe and missed. "I don't need to tell you anything."

"Oh, so you do have something to tell? I wondered."

Her face turned a deep shade of plum. "That's not what I meant."

"Then why did you run when you saw me?"

"Because I thought you might've broken your promise and told the cops about me."

"Good effort, Lyra, but I can tell you're lying. Your gaze shifts to the left when you lie. Did you also lie about what happened to you? Who told you to do that?" The master of the gwiber, perhaps?

"Nobody. I was attacked."

"Cut the bullshit, Lyra. I don't see an Oscar in your future. Who put you up to it? If I don't get an answer I believe this time, I'll haul you straight to Chief Garcia and let her sort it out."

Lyra crumbled like a gluten free cookie. "Okay, okay! I'll talk. Please don't torture me. My skin is really fair. A bruise on my face will last for weeks, and I have an audition coming up."

An audition. Lyra was an actress. "I'm waiting."

She clenched her jaw, clearly unhappy with her choices. "It was Penelope Bridger."

"Penelope Bridger cut you up and sent you to my house? Was there really a Theo?"

She shook her head. "No, it was all made up."

I recalled Sierra's locator spell to find Ashley. *But all I'm getting are the sounds around me.* So clever. She told the truth without giving anything away.

"What does Ashley have to do with the gwiber?"

Lyra pulled a face. "I don't know what that is. Is it some kind of fancy dog?"

I squeezed her shoulder. Hard.

"Ouch! I don't know anything about Ashley or a gwiber, okay? The Bridgers know I've been auditioning for roles in the city, so they offered me money to show up at your house and tell you that story."

I was so angry, I could've spit fire like Kane's chimera cat.

Lyra attempted to run past me but to no avail. I swept my leg toward hers and hooked my foot around her ankle. She stumbled to the ground. She stared at her hands in frustration. "This better not leave marks."

"Go straight home, Lyra. Do not go to the Bridger's farm. Do not call them." For good measure, I bent down and took her cell phone from her pocket. As she scrambled to her feet to reclaim it, I chucked it in the dumpster.

"Hey! I'm waiting to hear about an audition."

"You can come back and get it tomorrow." I regretted

having shown Lyra my tender side when she showed up at the Castle. I should've been more suspicious.

"Please don't tell them I told you," Lyra pleaded. "The old lady scares me. She's like a witch."

I grunted. "Isn't she just?"

I watched Lyra from the shadows to make sure she followed my orders. Then I debated my next move. The Bridger witches had Ashley, but why? And what did the gwiber have to do with them?

I glanced at the clear sky above and got my answer. The moon stared back at me, round and radiant. Not just a supermoon but a Strawberry Supermoon full of mystical energy in a town that was already jam-packed with it.

In other words, it was the perfect night for a sacrifice.

CHAPTER 18

I debated whether to call West for backup. In the end, I decided to go it alone. I'd never relied on anybody before, nor did I see the point in starting now. It would only endanger them and disappoint me. It would be a fool's errand to go without weapons though, which meant a pitstop at my house.

There was no sign of my ghostly neighbors as I bolted into the house and ran upstairs to my bedroom. I pulled out the chest from under my bed and filled a backpack with as many weapons as I could carry. A backpack wasn't the most practical choice, but I had no idea what to expect at the Bridger farm. Penelope had a shotgun, and the witches also had magic, presumably dark magic if they were kidnapping people and summoning creatures like the gwiber. I sheathed a dagger and attached it to my thigh for quick and easy access.

I drove my truck to the closest main intersection and parked. Of all the weapons in my pack, the element of surprise was the most crucial one. I covered the final half mile on foot, pausing only once to crouch behind a bush to avoid a set of headlights.

I'd researched the gwiber. What I hadn't expected was the

need to rescue Ashley and kill the beast at the same time. I'd considered them two separate actions.

I kept my head down as the farmhouse came into view. An interior light shone through the window of the front room. If my timing was right, the witches would still be inside preparing their materials for the ritual. There was, of course, the small matter of the ward that would alert them to my presence. I'd have to move swiftly.

I darted past the house and cut through the yard toward the outbuildings. The barn was the most likely place to stash Ashley until the time came to present her as an offering to the gwiber. My skin crawled at the thought of poor Ashley being served to the creature on a silver platter. They must've assumed there was no one who cared enough to search for her. My hands clenched into fists as I reached the barn doors. Locked.

I could handle that.

I kicked the seam of the doors and watched the wood shake. I wasn't as strong as supernaturals like West, but I could hold my own, especially against a barn door that hadn't been properly maintained in fifty years.

The doors crashed open, and I rushed through them. I skimmed the stalls, and my gaze landed on a body chained to a beam. Her head lolled to the side. Wisps of light brown hair stuck to her cheeks. I rushed forward and gently shook her.

"Ashley, are you awake?"

Her head rolled the other way, and I gasped when I recognized Phaedra's face. Why was Penelope's daughter chained in the barn?

I patted her cheeks firmly in an effort to rouse her. Her eyes blinked open, and she tried to focus.

"My head," she mumbled.

"Someone knocked you unconscious?"

She nodded groggily. "Key…"

"I don't see the key, but I'll find it."

"Stop them. I tried…"

I had a million questions but no time to ask them; there was only time for one. "Where is she?"

"Pond," she whispered, her voice hoarse. I didn't want to think why. As much as I hated to leave Phaedra chained in the barn, time was of the essence.

I dashed toward the backyard, nearly colliding with Brenda who'd emerged from a side door of the house clutching a wicker basket.

The witch stared at me in confusion. "You tripped the ward? Kelsey said it was a squirrel."

"Kelsey is an idiot."

Brenda swung the basket in the air, intending to hit me in the head. I tore the basket from her grasp and flung it into the bushes.

"We need those for the ritual!" she cried.

"There isn't going to be a ritual."

"You don't understand. It's the only way."

"The only way to murder innocent people. Yes, I agree."

I heard the telltale click and knew I'd wasted too much time.

"Don't turn around, and put your hands up," Penelope demanded.

Slowly I raised my hands. "You don't want to do this, Penelope. There's still time to change your mind." I paused. "I guess Phaedra did, which is why she's currently unconscious and chained up in the barn."

Brenda whirled around to face her sister. "You chained Phaedra in the barn? You said she was keeping an eye on Ashley."

"She was going to betray us," Penelope hissed. "I couldn't risk it."

"Betray us how?" Brenda asked.

Penelope tightened her grip on the shotgun. "We can talk about it later. Right now, we need to finish the preparations.

The Strawberry Supermoon is our best chance." She snarled at me. "Too bad you'll miss all the fun, you imbecile. Imagine coming here alone and expecting to stop us."

"Hot tip: names might hurt me, but buckshot won't." I grabbed the barrel of the shotgun and yanked it to the side, pulling Penelope with it. The gun fired, but the shot went wide, knocking the bark off a nearby tree.

It wasn't strictly true that buckshot couldn't hurt me; it just couldn't kill me.

I was complicated.

Using the butt of the shotgun, I shoved Penelope to the ground, then tossed the gun out of reach.

"Stop her," Penelope growled.

Brenda shot her a helpless look. "With what? She defeated my wicker basket."

I left them to argue and raced toward the pond. The stench of moonshine was stronger here. Maybe the witches had indulged themselves before the big moment. Liquid courage for the atrocity they were about to commit.

And, suddenly, there she was.

A wooden post protruded from the center of the pond and tied to that post was Ashley Pratt. It seemed pretty rich for a coven of witches to tie another woman to a stake with the intent to kill her. They'd dressed her in a golden chemise. The fabric shimmered in the moonlight, as if sewn from the light of a thousand stars. They wanted Ashley to be seen—so where was the gwiber?

A snapping sound interrupted my thoughts. I turned to see a gigantic crocodile-like creature lumber in Ashley's direction. Not a gwiber. Her scream could've split wood.

"Don't move," a voice yelled.

Kelsey had joined the other witches in the backyard, along with Sierra and Margaret.

"Let the beast feast on her flesh," Margaret added. "One human girl is worth the exchange."

Confusion flooded my mind as I kept my focus on the monster. Where was the gwiber? Even more concerning, what were the odds that Ashley would be terrorized by the Lake Placid type of creature that had given her nightmares in childhood?

Slim, that's what they were. Very slim.

There was no time to think it through. Right now, I had to get the monster's attention away from Ashley. I ripped an axe from my pack and threw it. The witches watched as it arced through the air, over the creature's long body.

"Ha! You missed," Kelsey said with a satisfied smile.

I twisted to face her. "I wasn't aiming for the creature."

Her smug expression evaporated when she saw where the blade of the axe landed. It sliced through one of Ashley's ropes, freeing her right hand.

The sight of the weapon seemed to anger the monster because it opened its massive jaws and released a deafening roar. The witches' hands slammed against their ears. The creature swiveled away from the pond and flattened itself on the ground.

"What's it doing?" Margaret asked. "Why is it facing us instead of the offering?"

"Because we didn't finish the preparation," Brenda moaned.

"It just needs a command." Kelsey ran directly into its path and jabbed an angry finger toward the pond. "She's behind you. That's your offering. Go take it!" She turned to face the others. "Maybe we need to say it in Spanish? Can anybody translate?"

"Phaedra could." Brenda faltered.

Kelsey shouldn't have turned her back to the creature. The crocodilian monster pounced on the redhead and swallowed her whole.

Brenda screamed. "Penelope, do something!"

"What do you think this sacrifice is for, you stupid cow? It won't obey me yet," Penelope barked. "Sierra, get rid of this nuisance."

This nuisance was currently having a moment of clarity. The sacrifice. The moonshine. The missing gwiber. The unlikely crocodile monster. Kelsey's seemingly ridiculous question about asking in Spanish.

"That's a culebrón," I announced to no one in particular. The culebrón was a shapeshifting monster associated with the rural Chilean countryside. It had a fondness for aguardiente, hence the moonshine, which may be how they summoned it, and its domestication was best achieved through sacrifice. Its regular form was a monster-sized hairy snake with the giant head of a calf, but the creature can shift into whatever form frightens children the most. Based on its current form, Ashley's inner child was still traumatized by crocodilian monsters.

"You will not ruin this for us," Penelope said. "The stars have finally aligned, and tonight we domesticate the culebrón."

"Why claim it as a pet? You can't exactly walk it around town on a leash." Then I remembered the other critical piece of information—a domesticated culebrón was capable of bringing wealth to its 'owner.' My stomach turned. Of all the reasons to sacrifice people. "This is about money?"

"We've sacrificed too much to let you stop us now." Margaret rushed forward to protect the culebrón. The creature showed its appreciation by opening its massive jaws and devouring the witch. Its mouth snapped closed, and I fought the revulsion that pushed its way through my insides. This wasn't a Jonah and the Whale situation. The creature wouldn't be vomiting out Kelsey and Margaret.

I wasn't sure when people stopped screaming; the sound had become background noise.

Tears streaked Brenda's face. "This has gone too far, Penelope. Too many lives have been lost already. What if the sacrifice fails to work again? Let her kill it before it kills the rest of us."

Again. There'd been other attempts. I'd bet good money Officer Lindley was one of them.

Penelope's face remained impassive. "Sierra, our visitor says buckshot can't hurt her. See if magic can."

Sierra's eyes flickered with uncertainty. She seemed torn between Brenda's good sense and Penelope's terrifying madness.

"I don't want to hurt you, Sierra," I warned, "but you lob a single spell at me, and you'll live to regret it."

While Sierra debated her unappealing options, the culebrón took the opportunity to change into its natural form. With bulging eyes and deformed ears, its head was grotesque, not at all like any calf I'd ever seen. Its serpentine body was covered in a layer of coarse hair.

"There you are, big fella," I said. "I bet it feels good to be back in your own skin." I felt a strange connection to the beast, knowing it could access the nightmares of its victims.

Screaming at the transformation, Sierra turned and ran. Wrong move. The culebrón was a predator, and Sierra just identified herself as prey.

"Sierra, no!" Brenda's cry came too late.

The culebrón shifted in the direction of the sound. Brenda didn't bother to run. She simply dropped to her knees and offered herself as a midnight snack to prevent the creature from chasing Sierra. It didn't work. The monster easily caught up to Sierra and gulped her down as a side dish.

Rage twisted Penelope's features. Her body twitched as she pointed a finger at me. "You'll pay for this."

"Yes, with the treasure my new pet manifests for me. At least these sacrifices won't be wasted, am I right?" Despite my bravado, I wasn't sure what magic Penelope was capable of. There was also the rather large matter of the culebrón…

A blackbird swooped down and landed on a nearby fencepost. I waved my hand in an effort to scare it away. No need to put itself in harm's way.

"You've taken everything from me." Penelope's voice shook with fury. "I won't let you take this gift too." The older witch charged at me. Unfortunately for her, the culebrón had decided to do the same from the opposite side. I jumped back and watched as the two of them collided, or more accurately, Penelope collided with the monster's mouth.

I heard the sound of clapping and looked over to see Kane. Wearing a crisp white shirt beneath a black suit, he seemed overdressed for the occasion. "A well-executed maneuver, Miss Clay. And a nod to the classics as well. I fully approve."

"The classics?"

"The Marx Brothers, or perhaps The Three Stooges, if your slapstick preferences lean more lowbrow."

I couldn't manage a snarky reply. Now that the monster had probably managed to pick its teeth with Penelope's bones, it had circled back to me.

"Don't you need a nap after such a big meal?" I asked. "You just had Thanksgiving and Christmas dinners rolled into one."

The monster roared. The force blew back my hair and covered my face in a fine mist that reeked of moonshine.

"You seem to be struggling, Miss Clay." Kane's tone suggested mild amusement. What a prick.

"I'm fine, thanks for asking." I reached into my backpack and slowly retrieved a three-pointed star, keeping one eye trained on the monster. I let it fly, and the curved points became a blur. The star stuck in the monster's neck but seemed to have no effect.

"Are you certain a mortal weapon can kill it?" Kane asked mildly. "Perhaps it requires something more potent."

"Don't know." Grunting, I hurled another throwing axe at the monster's head. The blade wedged itself into the beast's forehead, yet it remained unfazed. "But, so far, they haven't had much impact." All those previous sacrifices had likely strengthened the culebrón.

On the ground about twenty feet away, a metal fragment glimmered in the moonlight. I ran for the shotgun left by Penelope. As the monster bore down on me, I fired. The noise startled the creature, which bought me enough time to fire again. A shotgun wasn't the most efficient weapon. My guess was that Penelope had only ever intended to use it on humans.

Kane continued to observe me from a safe distance. "You strike me as an educated woman. I'm going to assume you're familiar with the definition of insanity."

"I am."

"Then why in the devil's name are you continuing to use mortal weapons to try and kill it? Seems counterproductive, no?"

"He's right," Ashley said, her voice trembling.

My head jerked toward her. "Hey, who's the one trying to rescue you? He's just standing over there." Looking ridiculously handsome and smug, throwing around his big demon energy, but I refused to say that part out loud.

As much as I wanted to thump Kane in the head with my next weapon, he was right. Nothing I did seemed to weaken the culebrón. If only ancient myths were more precise with their information, especially as it pertained to killing monsters, it would save us modern folks a lot of time and trouble.

I realized Ashley was still struggling to free her other hand. "Sir, would you mind helping me escape while the lady's busy fighting?"

Nana Pratt would be proud of Ashley's ability to be polite even in the heat of battle. Kane, on the other hand, seemed momentarily confused by the request.

"In case you haven't noticed, there's a rather large monster between us," Kane called to her.

"Why are you here if you don't intend to help?" I asked. He was a powerful demon; there was no doubt he'd be an asset. Then it occurred to me. Kane wasn't here out of the goodness of his heart. He was here to see what I could do. He thought if he watched me fight, he'd be able to figure out exactly who or what I am.

Nice try, demon. Nothing about this fight will reveal my true identity. I was going old school.

I unsheathed my dagger and ran toward my opponent. The culebrón raised its enormous calf-like head, and I slid beneath it, slicing its throat open as I skimmed the ground. Black liquid dripped from the wound.

In pain, the creature flicked its serpentine body to the side, allowing me to glide past it and straight back to my feet.

"It's only a flesh wound," Kane called out. Funny.

I glanced over to the pond to see that he'd freed Ashley and was now standing at the water's edge dripping wet. He'd removed his suit jacket and his white shirt stuck to his torso, revealing a solid set of abs, not that I had any doubt they existed.

I clung to the monster in an effort to climb on its hairy back. The creature's slick body made it difficult to gain purchase, but I finally made it, despite the undulation of the culebrón's back as it tried to dislodge me.

Rolling up his sleeves, Kane advanced toward us.

"Stay back!" I didn't want anybody else in the danger zone.

"I thought you wanted help."

"I don't want to have to rescue you."

It was hard to tell in the dim light, but I was pretty sure he smirked. "Here. Take this. You've earned it." He held up his hand, which began to burn with a white light.

"Um, Kane. Your hand is on fire."

The light extended into a blade. It took mere seconds for the flaming sword to fully form, and he tossed it to me as readily as a coin.

"You're a man of hidden talents." Except he wasn't a man at all, and it was best to remember that.

I snatched the sword from the air by the hilt and jammed the white-hot blade into the fleshy part of the culebrón's neck, where its calf head met its snake body.

"Excellent reflexes," Kane remarked. He'd carried Ashley across the pond and stood at the water's edge, still holding her.

I slid to the ground as the culebrón collapsed on its side. The flame of the sword dissipated, as though it sensed the deed was done. "I'm especially good at sucker punches. Care to test me?"

"I'll take your word for it." He set Ashley down and retrieved his jacket from where he'd hung it on the fencepost.

I crossed the yard and returned the hilt of the sword to him. "How did you conjure this thing?"

The amber in his whisky-colored eyes intensified. "I'll tell you mine if you tell me yours."

I was so distracted that I missed where he put the sword. Did it fit in his pocket? Melt into his skin? Damn mesmerizing eyes.

"Not a chance."

"I can't thank you enough for saving me," Ashley said.

I pivoted to face her. It was a miracle she was unharmed. Nana Pratt never would've forgiven me if I failed to rescue her.

"How did you know what that thing was?" Ashley asked.

I glanced at what was left of the flaming carcass. "Let's just say I know a thing or two about living nightmares." I dipped my hand into my front pocket. "I believe this belongs to you."

Tears filled Ashley's eyes. "My bracelet."

"Steven loaned it to me to help find you."

A quiet gasp escaped her. "My brother asked you to find me?"

"He's been so worried, Ashley. He never gave up hope."

She threw her arms around my neck and squeezed me to the point of choking. I quickly extricated myself from her uncomfortable embrace. It was awkward enough being hugged by people I knew; strangers were on another level.

"Hey, Kane, would you mind making yourself useful and escorting Ashley home? You know where she lives."

"I believe I made myself useful more than once this evening."

Despite his words, he covered Ashley with his suit jacket. "We'll take the Bridgers' vehicle," he said. "They certainly won't be needing it anytime soon."

I could think of one Bridger who might. As they walked away, I returned to the barn to free Phaedra. The witch was fully awake now, although the pained expression on her face suggested a massive headache—and heartache.

She directed me to the key, and I unlocked the chains. Once free, she collapsed in a grateful heap. "I heard the commotion, but I couldn't tell what was happening. Did you save her?"

"Yes."

She rubbed her wrists. "I didn't know until today, I swear. I would've told you before, when you were here."

"I believe you."

Phaedra leaned her head against the wooden post. "They started with a Jin Chan."

"What's that?"

"Basically a money frog. It was supposed to attract wealth."

"Did it?"

"We won the lottery. It wasn't very much though. Mother was furious. When they told me the stupid frog ate the turtles in the pond, I was devastated, but I knew the farm needed money, so I let it go."

"What happened to the frog?"

"It got eaten by something bigger."

"The culebrón?"

"Yes. The frog was Mother's first sacrifice. After she summoned the culebrón, she thought offering a sacred mythological creature would be enough to tame it, so it would bring us money." She paused. "Is it dead?"

"Yes."

Her mouth formed a thin line. "Good. I was so horrified when they told me what they'd been doing. They weren't even ashamed. They said it like it was the most natural thing in the world, to sacrifice people for their own personal gain." She grimaced. "Georgia was my friend. She worked here for years."

"Georgia? The brownie?"

She nodded. "It ate all the other animals too. And Officer Lindley. That one hadn't been planned. The culebrón had broken through the ward again and escaped. Officer Lindley spotted it in the woods at the same time Mother and Aunt Brenda tracked it down. Mother took the opportunity to make use of her."

"That's how her blood ended up in the woods."

Phaedra wiped a tear from her cheek. "Mother left it there on purpose. She thought it would help with the animal attack theory that was being spread around."

"And then Ashley happened to cross their path?"

"Kelsey was at Monk's and saw Ashley talking to a guy she liked. He was about thirty-five, and it enraged Kelsey that he'd be hitting on someone Ashley's age."

"But instead of taking it out on him, she decided to take it out on Ashley."

"Two birds, one stone, as far as Kelsey was concerned. We had a ready-made sacrifice for the Strawberry Supermoon, which Mother said would guarantee domestication. She decided the previous full moons lacked the necessary power." Phaedra felt for the bump on her head. "It was Kelsey who knocked me out and chained me up. She always does Mother's bidding." Phaedra struggled to her feet.

"What about Anya Swanson? Was she just a diversion?"

Phaedra nodded. "Yes. Mother hates vampires. She was determined to keep the focus on them, at least until after the sacrifice tonight."

"Well, there was a sacrifice. Just not the one they intended."

Her face contorted. "Are they all dead?"

I nodded. "I'm sorry."

Phaedra clamped a hand over her mouth and stifled a cry.

"It happened quickly, if it helps."

Her eyes misted over. "But Ashley is okay."

"She is. Can I ask why you were away all those months?"

"I'd been unhappy here for most of my life," she admitted. "I didn't like the way my family talked about humans, like they were walking pieces of garbage. I worried it was me, that maybe I was too sensitive." She bit her lower lip. "That's what Mother always said anyway, that I was too sensitive. That I cared too much about creatures that were inferior to us."

"So, you wanted to create distance between you."

Phaedra wiped a runaway tear. "I figured if I spent time away, with other people, that I might get a different perspective." She paused. "And, boy, did I."

"Why come home then? Why not stay away?"

"Because I thought I could change them. Foolish, I know. How could I expect to undo a lifetime of damage?"

"You tried, and that's the important part."

"Not hard enough. They're dead now, and so are other innocent people. Maybe I could've stopped it."

"You did try to stop it, remember? That's how you ended up in here." And it saved her life.

Phaedra closed her eyes. "The beast is gone. At least that will make running the farm easier."

"Are you sure you'll want to stay? This is a big place for one woman."

She smiled at me. "It is. Got any tips?"

I slid an arm underneath her and helped her to the house. "Will you be okay on your own?" I asked, as she opened the kitchen door.

"Yes, thank you. For everything. I'm in your debt."

I walked back to the pond to dispose of the monster's corpse. I was relieved none of the witches' spirits appeared before me. I wasn't in the mood to deal with their ghosts.

Kane stood with his hands in his pockets, assessing the scene as though admiring a painting in a gallery.

"How did you get back here so quickly?"

"Demon speed," he said vaguely.

"Where was that demon speed when the fight started? Nice of you to show up at the last possible minute, by the way," I said.

"You told me to stay back."

I arched an eyebrow. "And you listened?"

"You're welcome."

I gave him a long look. "I didn't know you carried a concealed weapon."

"There's a lot you don't know about me."

"I know that you carry a cool sword."

"I don't carry it. It's mystical. Comes and goes at will."

"Its will or yours?"

"Mine." His gaze raked over me. I must've looked very glamorous, with guts in my hair and blood smudges on my cheek. "Who taught you how to fight monsters?"

"I was born female. It comes with the ovaries."

Kane smiled at that. "I don't think fighting the culebrón is quite the same."

I arched an eyebrow. "Are you sure you run a nightclub?"

"I wouldn't have expected you to become so invested in one mortal girl."

"I told you; I made a deal with her brother."

"Yes, but what you're denying to yourself is that you cared." He cocked his head, assessing me. "You cared whether Ashley lived or died. You didn't want her to be sacrificed."

"And you did?" I rolled my eyes. "Oh, wait. I forgot who I was talking to. Of course you didn't care. You're a big, bad demon with a heart of coal. You only intervened for the sake of business."

He ignored me. "You care because Ashley could've been you. A young woman who slipped through the cracks of society and met an untimely demise."

"Ashley didn't deserve the gruesome fate that the witches intended for her. She's made mistakes, but nothing so bad that she can't come back from."

"The witches won't be coming back from their mistake, I see." Kane observed the creature's corpse. "I'm surprised it hasn't dissolved into black goo or something equally horrible."

"Help me push it into the pond."

"That's your plan? Contaminate the water supply with mystical germs?"

"Do you have a better one? I can't exactly call the police."

"I'll take care of it," he said.

My eyebrows inched up. "You will?"

"I have demons in my service that will make short work of this." He waved a hand airily at the large body.

I decided it was best not to know the details. "What's in it for you?"

He frowned, as though the answer surprised him. "Absolutely nothing."

CHAPTER 19

Nana Pratt tried to hug me ten times before she gave up. I felt the whoosh of air as her arms sliced through me.

"I get it; you're grateful," I told her. "You can stop trying to show me." I'd barely passed through the gate to the Castle when Nana Pratt and Ray pounced for news on Ashley. Nana didn't even comment on my current unseemly condition.

"As much as I want to see my Ashley again, I don't want to see her on this side of things," Nana Pratt said. "Did she say when she'll come by to say hello?"

"Give her a chance to recover first. She's pretty traumatized by the whole ordeal." I figured I'd let Steven tell his sister the details of her rescue, the ones he knew anyway.

"Did you know about the crossroads?" I asked, unlocking the front door.

"The what?" Ray asked.

I pushed open the door. "Never mind. You've never heard of people going missing from Fairhaven?" If what Kane told me was true, it wouldn't surprise me to learn there'd been hundreds of incidents over the years.

"I've heard tales of people going missing. UFOs in the

mountains and that sort of thing," Nana Pratt said. I noticed that she and Ray remained on the porch even though I was now inside.

"Why didn't you mention it in relation to Ashley?" I asked.

Her eyes widened incredulously. "Do you think I believed any of it?"

"You assumed people left of their own accord, the same way other people believe Ashley ran away."

She nodded. "Now, of course, I see things differently."

I bet she did.

"Why doesn't anybody do anything about it?" Nana Pratt lamented. "If there's a long history of disappearances, it seems to me something ought to be done."

"What do you recommend?" I asked, not unkindly. "Most of you don't believe the people are truly missing, and most of you don't know about the crossroads or the supernatural world. So, what's the solution?"

Nana's gaze dropped to the lines in the floorboards. "I see your point."

"If you don't mind, I'm going to shower and go straight to bed."

The ghosts crowded in the doorway. "Do what you need to, dear," Nana Pratt said.

I slept like the dead. By the time I awoke, the sun was high in the sky. Despite my aching muscles, I felt rested, which was a good thing because I had work to do today. I'd fallen woefully behind thanks to Ashley.

I scrambled eggs and added spinach and feta because I was feeling fancy. I washed it down with hot tea. I spent the day with my headphones on and music blasting in my ears as I tackled the downstairs half bath. I cleared my mind of recent events and focused only on the task in front of me. It felt good.

The ward alerted me to another visitor. I glanced out the

window to see Chief Garcia saunter across the bridge toward the Castle. She paused to peer down at the moat before continuing to the house. Grabbing a nearby broom, I opened the front door and intercepted her on the porch under the guise of coming outside to sweep.

"Chief Garcia, what a nice surprise. Welcome to the Castle."

She squinted at the monstrosity behind me. "I guess it's the interior you're working on."

"Those rooms won't make themselves habitable."

She smirked. "No, I suppose they won't."

I leaned on the broom handle. "What brings you here?"

"I wanted to say thank you for finding Ashley. This town owes you a debt of gratitude."

"Not at all. Steven and I had a deal." And we'd now fulfilled our obligations to each other.

Her brow creased. "I didn't realize the Bridger farm was a religious cult. I don't know how I missed it. It seems so obvious now, when I think about it."

"The Bridger family has lived on that land for generations. They were white noise to the people of Fairhaven. I was able to see them for what they were because I saw them through a pair of fresh eyes. I have no history with them."

She nodded. "That's a good point. I spent more time reviewing your background than I did thinking about anybody else's."

"I understand why you did though."

The chief cast a glance over her shoulder. "The parade is happening later today, if you're up for it."

"Parade?"

"Fourth of July. I know you lived in England for a few years, but I don't think your friends there would be offended if you partook in any festivities to celebrate our independence from them."

I smiled. "No, I'm sure they wouldn't." If I had any.

"You're a natural, you know. The way you ran your investigation. You should consider a new career."

"I have my hands full at the moment, but thanks for the vote of confidence." I made a show of sweeping the debris off the porch.

"You won't find enough lost heirs in this area to continue your practice here," she pressed. "Might as well apply those skills another way."

I didn't react. I could tell she had more to say.

"That was a big case you landed," she continued, proving me right. "The Allthorpe estate. There was so much money involved that it made the papers."

"It was a huge windfall," I agreed.

"Better than the lottery, really, because you found that lord's missing heir. Were they annoyed to have to share a percentage of the estate with you?"

"No, they were grateful. If I hadn't found them, they would never have known about the inheritance." And they'd needed the money. Lord Allthorpe's cousin was fighting cancer and had been interested in trying alternative treatments but couldn't afford them. The inheritance bought him the most precious resource in the world—time. And I was using my portion to do the same.

Chief Garcia nodded. "I'm interviewing replacements for Officer Lindley. In the meantime, if I need someone to bounce ideas off of, would you mind if I paid you a visit?"

"I doubt you'll need me again. Fairhaven isn't exactly the crime capital of Pennsylvania."

"No, but we get more than our share of incidents."

I stopped sweeping. "I'm sure there are more suitable people in town."

She held up her hands in acquiescence. "I get it. You're not interested. You came here for peace and quiet."

"I did."

"Well, you won't be getting it tonight. The fireworks are noisy, but you'll have a great view of them from here."

I followed her gaze to the town below and the hint of the river beyond. It didn't need fireworks to be beautiful. It was picturesque exactly as it was.

"I appreciate you coming to see me, Chief. I'm sure I'll see you around."

She tapped her badge. "I'm hard to miss." She turned on her heel and retraced her steps across the bridge, pausing again to look at the moat. "You might want to throw some chemicals in there. You've got a buildup of bacteria. You wouldn't want to pick up a flesh-eating virus from your own moat."

"No, but I'd like my enemies to."

She frowned, as though not quite sure whether I was joking. I offered a friendly final wave and resumed sweeping.

"She thinks you're a real asset," Ray surmised, observing the chief as she climbed into the driver's seat of her SUV.

"Because she *is* a real asset," Nana Pratt said.

I left the broom on the porch and retreated inside, away from the sweltering heat. "I'm not an asset. I'm a person."

"Not quite a person, though, are you?" Nana remarked.

I refused to respond or even look at her. I didn't want to have this conversation. I needed no reminders of who I really was. I knew perfectly well; I'd been running from it my whole life.

"I didn't give you permission to enter the house," I told them. "If you keep breaking the rules, you know what happens."

They exchanged fearful glances.

"You wouldn't," Nana said in a low voice. "We're friends now."

I didn't respond. I returned to my work, stopping occasionally to eat and drink. When I finally finished, I treated myself to a homemade cheeseburger and a beer. I gobbled down the food, polished off the beer, and swiped a second bottle from the fridge to carry to the front porch. Darkness had fallen. The show was about to start.

I spotted the blackbird on the iron finial of the gate, standing sentry again. I raised my beer bottle in salute. The bird cawed and turned to face the town.

I sat on the front step, drinking my beer, and watched as fireworks exploded in the sky. Red, white, and blue to mark the occasion. I pictured the parade below; the children riding their bicycles along the main street. The marching band following behind them playing patriotic tunes. I wasn't one for nationalism, but I enjoyed the existence of traditions. It made people feel safe and comfortable, like they belonged. I got that.

"They sure are pretty," Nana Pratt remarked, appearing beside me.

"It's a good show this year," Ray agreed, appearing on the other side of me. "Last year, Ronnie Whittaker lost two fingers setting off the fireworks. I thought we might not have them this year."

"They hired someone to coordinate the parade this year," Nana Pratt said.

"You should've gone down there, Lorelei," Ray said. "Would've been a good opportunity to meet more of the locals."

"She's met plenty," Nana Pratt shot back. "She must've met half the town looking for my Ashley."

"I'm all peopled out," I told them. "I'm perfectly content to watch the theatrics from here."

I leaned back against the step and admired the colorful display. The last time I watched fireworks was Bonfire Night in England two years ago. I'd been huddled in a crowd, feeling stifled but warm in my heavy coat. It had been an exceptionally cold November night. I'd enjoyed myself until the spirits found me, as they always did.

I swilled the last of the beer. The fireworks resembled stars raining down from the sky.

"Happy Independence Day, Lorelei," Ray said.

I set the empty bottle beside me. I wouldn't say I was free, but I was close enough.

Don't miss **Dead of Night**, the next book in the *Crossroads Queen* series.

To join my VIP list and download an extended scene from Kane's POV in Chapter 6, visit https://annabelchase.com/dead-to-the-world-offer.

OTHER SERIES BY ANNABEL CHASE

Midnight Empire series

Pandora's Pride

Federal Bureau of Magic

Starry Hollow Witches

Magic Bullet

Spellbound/Spellbound Ever After

Spellslingers Academy

Demonspawn Academy

The Bloomin' Psychic

Divine Place

Midlife Magic Cocktail Club

Hex Support

Printed in Great Britain
by Amazon